NEW ORLEANS
Battle of the Bayous

Harry Albright

HIPPOCRENE BOOKS
New York

27296

Acknowledgments

Chief sources consulted in writing this study of the towering career of
Andrew Jackson and the great battle that exploded him onto the world
stage include *The Life of Andrew Jackson* by Marquis James, the Bobbs-
Merrill Company, 1938; *The British at the Gates* by Robin Reilly, G. P.
Putnam's Sons, 1974; *The Age of Jackson* by Arthur M. Schlesinger, Jr.,
Little, Brown and Company, 1953; *Andrew Jackson—Soldier and Statesman*
by Ralph K. Andrist, The American Heritage Publishing Company,
1963; and *Andrew Jackson 1767—1845*, edited by Ronald E. Shaw, Oceana
Publications, Inc., 1969.

I extend my thanks to the following libraries for their help in gathering information for this book: Tripler Army Hospital Library, Fort
Shafter Army Library and the Aina Haina Public Library in Honolulu.

Hippocrene paperback edition, 1991

For information, contact
Hippocrene Books, Inc.
171 Madison Avenue
New York, NY 10016

Library of Congress Cataloging-in-Publication Data

Albright, Harry.
  New Orleans : battle of the bayous / Harry Albright.
    p.   cm.
  ISBN 0-87052-878-5
  1. New Orleans, Battle of, 1814.   2. Jackson, Andrew, 1767–1845-
-Military leadership.   I. Title.
  E356.N5A53   1990
  973.5'239—dc20   90-42627
                                                          CIP

ISBN 0-87052-007-5

Printed in the United States of America.

*To Carolyn, Elizabeth,
Catherine and Michael*

Contents

Part IV   *Before one month the British and Spanish forces expect to be in Possession of Mobile and all the surrounding country. There will be bloody noses before this happens.*
    —Jackson to his ward, Robert Butler,
    on August 27, 1814

Part V   *Whoever is not for us, is against us.*
    —General Andrew Jackson to Louisiana
    Governor Claiborne, December 1814

Part VI   *You must not sleep until you reach me.*
    —General Jackson to General John Coffee
    at Baton Rouge, December 15, 1814

Part VII   *Gentlemen, the British are below. We must fight them tonight.*
    —Andrew Jackson at his headquarters,
    December 23, 1814

Part VIII   *Pakenham, who distrusted the proceedings of Sir Alexander Cochrane, showed great anxiety on the voyage to arrive at the scene of operations before his troops had been put on shore.*

                                        —Lieutenant Colonel John Fox Burgoyne

Part IX   *That fatal ever fatal rocket.*

                        —British officer before American line at
                                        New Orleans, January 8, 1815

Part X   *. . . they crowned him with laurel. The Lord has promised his humble followers a crown that fadeth not away; the present one is already withered the leaves falling off. . . . Pray for your sister in a heathen land.*

                                        —Rachel Jackson, New Orleans

Part XI   *Our Union: It must be preserved!*

                        —Toast by President Jackson, April 13, 1830

Part XII   *The bank is trying to kill me, but I will kill it!*
                              —Jackson to Van Buren, July 3, 1832

Part XIII   *Thou great democratic God! Thou who didst pick
                up Andrew Jackson from the pebbles; who didst
                hurl him upon a warhorse; who didst thunder him
                higher than a throne.*
                              —Herman Melville in *Moby Dick*

Part I

There is a certain blend of courage, character and principle which has no satisfactory dictionary name but has been called different things at different times in different countries. Our American name for it is "guts."

—Louis Adamic

1

The Muddy Boots

"**C**LEAN MY BOOTS!"

The arrogant command rang imperiously against the walls of the small room confining the two young Americans facing the angry British officer, elegant in his coat of scarlet and gold.

When the pair did not obey quickly enough, his saber was drawn from its scabbard and waved menacingly above their heads.

Fourteen-year-old Andrew Jackson answered defiantly for himself and his older brother, Robert.

"We will not do so. We are prisoners of war and must be treated as such."

Furiously, the king's officer smashed the saber down, cutting the boy's upraised left hand to the bone and scarring his head for life. He then turned his sword on Robert and wounded him seriously.

With blood running down their faces and onto their clothes, they were led away to jail.

Andrew would recover. Robert would die.

But the brutal treatment would live with Andrew the rest of his life.

The pair, along with other Revolutionary patriots, had been captured by raiding British cavalry.

The place was Waxsaws, on the border of North and South Carolina. The time was April 1781.

Shortly afterward, Jackson's widowed mother would die, leaving him to be raised by his mother's family, the Crawfords.

After teaching school and studying law, he rode westward to Nashville, Tennessee, where he set up a successful law practice and became a prominent figure in the military forces defending against the Indian raids along the long frontier. He became so prominent that he was to eventually be named a major general of the Tennessee militia.

In the meantime he had represented Tennessee in the national congress and, as a result of his blazing temper, had acquired a regional reputation as a duelist.

At least two of the duels would be fought over the good name of his wife, Rachel.

But that is a love story.

2

Romance on the River

WHEN ANDREW JACKSON ARRIVED AT THE PRIMITIVE frontier settlement of Nashville to become its first public prosecutor in a log courthouse surrounded by a distillery, two taverns, two stores and attendant log cabins, he experienced difficulty in finding a place to live.

The taverns were out.

They usually were filled with the people he was prosecuting.

The distillery would not have been proper.

So he finally took rooms at Widow Donelson's farm, ten miles outside of town.

There he met Widow Donelson's married daughter, Rachel Robards, pretty and with a mind of her own. She was back home with her mother because her jealous husband had made life in Kentucky miserable for her.

But miserable himself, her husband soon came from Kentucky to take her back with him. She went.

Soon, however, she sent word to her family that life with Robards was becoming impossible, and asked that they come and get her. But as the journey involved a traverse of hostile Indian country, her brothers asked Jackson to fulfill the mission.

He did so with the result that Robards sued for divorce, charging that she had eloped with Andrew Jackson.

Meanwhile, Jackson had found other lodgings removed from the Donelson farm.

Robards again showed up at the farm to pester Rachel to return to Kentucky, while directing threats at Jackson for his role in the marital discord. Jackson went to him and told him to desist or he would cut off his ears.

At this time Rachel decided to escape all her troubles by taking a flatboat trip down the Cumberland, Ohio and Mississippi Rivers to Natchez, but the flatboat captain would not take an unescorted woman as a passenger. So Jackson went along.

Leaving her with her friends in Natchez, Jackson returned to Nashville by way of the dangerous Natchez Trace.

There he found a surprise.

Robards was suing for divorce.

Jackson thought the legislature had granted it.

But he was wrong. The legislature had only granted Robards permission to bring his case before a court.

Nevertheless, the impetuous Jackson already was on his way back to Rachel in Natchez with the good news. They were married in Natchez in August 1791 and honeymooned in Mississippi before returning to Nashville to settle down on their own plantation on the Cumberland River.

It was a happy time, for it was a real love match.

But then shock!

In December 1793 Jackson learned that Robards' divorce

had been granted only three months earlier. He and Rachel had been living together illegally for two years.

Immediately they were married again, but the news was out all over the frontier.

Jackson got out his dueling pistols to put them in good order, for he knew he was bound to use them.

And he did.

3

Instant General

ACTIVE IN THE TENNESSEE MILITIA BOTH AS A JUDGE ADVO-
cate and a participant in the numerous skirmishes to
put down Indian raids, Jackson developed a great interest
in things military.

It was only natural that sooner or later his name would
be put forward to be elected general. But it was not to be,
for the then governor of Tennessee, Revolutionary War
hero John Sevier, would not approve his appointment.
However, in 1802 Jackson outmaneuvered his old political
opponent to capture the militia post with the rank of major
general.

He was yet to fight his first real battle.

One battle he did fight was a deadly duel with a detrac-
tor of Rachel.

This young man with a loose tongue and the reputation

of being one of the finest pistol shots in Tennessee was challenged by the furious Jackson in May 1806.

Charles Dickinson thought it would be an easy encounter, for in spite of his hair-trigger temper that embroiled him in much trouble, Jackson was not renowned as a great marksman.

When they turned to face each other at the command, "You may fire, gentlemen!", Dickinson shot first.

Jackson did not fall, but lifted his pistol.

His terror-stricken opponent was forced to wait through the agony of one misfire until Jackson, taking his time, finally levelled his pistol and fired.

Dickinson fell, fatally wounded.

Only when they had left the Kentucky dueling grounds did Jackson's seconds have to catch him when he fainted, for Dickinson's shot had lodged in his body, barely missing his heart. He would carry the bullet for the rest of his life.

But he still was defiant, and said, "I would have fired the same way if the bullet had gone through my brain."

4

Aborted Mission

THE STORMY LIFE OF ANDREW JACKSON WAS BECOMING mirrored in the increasing troubles of his country, which was caught in the gigantic struggle between Great Britain and her allies and Napoleon and his continental satellites.

But before this conflict had broken wide open, the great dictator, in search of funds for his continental armies, had sold the wide-spreading lands of the Louisiana territories to the United States.

Britain did not approve, but there was little that she could do. But she did rule the seas with the largest fleet the world had ever seen.

After 1805, when the British destroyed Napoleon's French and Spanish fleets at Trafalgar, she instituted a blockade of all Europe—and woe to the innocent by-

11

stander who got in the way of the proceedings. The United States was that bystander, and she got hurt. Her ships and cargoes were seized either by the British or the French as the case suited. Her seamen were impressed into the Royal Navy without a never-you-mind to serve the manpower needs of the fleet.

Then matters came to a head when the unready American frigate *Chesapeake* was stopped by the British frigate *Leopard* outside of Norfolk, Virginia, fired upon and forced to give up four of her crew to the Englishmen. There were dead and wounded seamen aboard the *Chesapeake* and the national outcry was tremendous.

But President Thomas Jefferson did not want war, so he smoothed matters over until he could turn the government over to James Madison early in 1809.

With United States drifting slowly toward war with Britain, a strange political paralysis gripped the nation.

Although the major complaints against the English were the impressment of American seamen and the seizure of American ships and cargoes by the men-of-war of the Royal Navy blockading Europe, the maritime states of New England were opposed to a war that would end seaborne trade completely.

Instead it was the frontier states of the West and those of the South that cried for action.

The reason: these states expected an easy conquest of Canada and a more rapid opening of the frontier lands on their western borders.

President Madison, knowing that the nation was woefully unprepared for armed conflict, tried his best to plot a course between Great Britain and Napoleon, which would preserve the country's honor and avoid war.

He failed.

When the conflict opened on June 18, 1812, it almost immediately became unpopularly known as "Mr. Madison's War."

Across the mountains in Tennessee, Major General Andrew Jackson offered the services of his 2,500 militiamen for an advance northward to Quebec. His message was politely received and filed.

There would seem to be no need for the impulsive general and his frontier troops in this war. Bitterly disappointed, there was nothing left for Jackson but to await the turn of events. They were not long in coming.

First would be the long-heralded invasion of Canada.

What was supposed to be a cakewalk into the northern territories immediately turned sour.

Fort Michilimackinac, on an island controlling the straits between Lakes Michigan and Huron, caught the first blow on July 17 when the commanding lieutenant looked out of the log-walled post to find himself besieged by about 500 British and Indians. He didn't have a chance, so he surrendered his eighty men without firing a shot.

He didn't even know there was a war on.

Far to the south at Fort Detroit, his superior, Brigadier General William Hull, was facing the same situation. British Major General Isaac Brock, commanding the king's forces in Upper Canada, demanded that he surrender or else face a massacre by Brock's Indian allies.

Hull gave in.

On August 16 he surrendered 2,200 troops, 2,500 muskets, cannon and the war brig *Adams*.

The same day the troops of the tiny American outpost at Fort Dearborn on the Chicago River, far to the west, were massacred by Potawatomi Indians.

The American army of the west had vanished.

At Forts Niagara and Erie, American expeditions into Canada likewise ended in utter failure.

Only one thrust remained.

Major General Henry Dearborn, senior general in the United States Army, was supposed to proceed up Lake Champlain and then descend on Montreal. He barely moved beyond the head of the lake and then went into winter quarters.

Fiasco.

There would be no more land actions in 1812.

A dismayed and irate country could only take heart in the superb achievements of the small but professional navy, whose powerful frigates emerged victorious over the Royal Navy in a number of single-ship actions.

But on the land, where defeat ruled the north, American eyes turned southward where the British had been stirring the fighting braves of the Indian nations to make war along the frontier.

The governor of Tennessee was called upon to provide 1,500 men for action along the border with Spanish Florida.

Jackson was eager to go, but there was an obstacle.

Jackson would have to serve under General James Wilkinson of the Regular Army who, although he, too, would fail on the Canadian frontier, was now commanding the offensive against Florida.

Jackson knew of the man's reputation, but he swallowed hard and agreed to serve under him in the campaign. Wilkinson, one of the senior generals in the army, had a checkered career that included involvement in the Conway Cabal directed against General George Washington in the Revolution, the scandals surrounding Aaron Burr in the Southwest, and possible collaboration with Spain when he was serving on the southern frontier.

The fledgling major general who had never fought a battle or led a campaign, nevertheless moved fast. By January 7, 1813, he had 2,000 militiamen on their way to Natchez on the Mississippi, infantry and artillery aboard flatboats that would proceed down the Cumberland, Ohio and Mississippi Rivers, and the cavalry proceeding overland along the Natchez Trace.

Andrew Jackson was learning about war fast.

But when he arrived at Natchez, he was due for some nasty surprises.

First, he received orders from Wilkinson to go into camp at Natchez and await further instructions.

After an impatient month he got them.

They were to disband his force, as the Florida campaign would be abandoned.

Dismissal of his troops eight hundred miles from home with no money, no food and no transportation was unthinkable. Jackson refused to obey. He would take his men home even if they had to walk.

And walk they did, except for the cavalry under his great friend, Colonel John Coffee, and the sick who rode in wagons Jackson had purchased out of his own personal funds.

Jackson himself? He walked. Even walking, he was all over the long column from the head to the tail, so much so that an admiring soldier said to his companion, "That Andy Jackson, he's tough." Someone in the column agreed, "You bet he's tough! Tough as hickory!"

So it wasn't long before the commanding general had a new name: "Old Hickory!"

His men loved him for taking care of them. They would take care of him.

Home in Nashville, Jackson, although ill, wrote to Washington and demanded a new command.

But he would have to fight another duel first.

The quarrel would arise from Jackson's action as a second to William Carroll, one of his officers on the Natchez expedition, in a duel with Jesse Benton, younger brother of Thomas Hart Benton, later to become senator from Missouri.

Carroll wounded Jesse Benton in the seat of his pants, to the vast amusement of the western frontier.

The Bentons were furious over Jackson's part in the affair.

They got their chance in Nashville in an affray in which Jackson was the only one wounded. He took a bullet from Jesse Benton's pistol in his left shoulder, before his old commander of cavalry, John Coffee, could extricate him.

Late in 1813, while Jackson lay in bed convalescing, word came up from southern Alabama that a war party of a thousand Creek braves had massacred hundreds of men, women and children at Fort Mims on the Alabama River.

It was his call to action.

Part II

The health of your general is restored. He will command in person.
—Andrew Jackson, September 24, 1813

5

Indian War

LISTENING TO REPORTS OF THE HORRORS OF FORT MIMS from his sickbed, Jackson smashed his fist down. "By the eternal these people must be saved!"

Looking up into the faces of his fellow Tennesseans, concerned for the safety of the long frontier, he lifted his head from his pillow. "The health of your general is restored. He will command in person."

Colonel John Coffee began assembling his cavalry.

Governor Blount approved of the mounting of an expedition of 2,500 men.

Old Hickory pledged that he would lead that column south within nine days.

And he did.

While he was recuperating from his wound, Jackson did a lot of hard thinking about the aborted Natchez expedition. While it had come to no profitable end, it had furnished Old Hickory with his first real education in the handling of a large body of soldiers in the field.

Without any formal military training of any kind, he had supervised the mobilization of the Tennessee troops, the supply of their arms, equipment and provision of food and ammunition.

Managing the dangerous flatboat voyage down the ice-choked Cumberland, Ohio and Mississippi Rivers in the dead of winter had proven to be no small feat of arms.

The futile month of indecisive waiting at Natchez followed by the unexpected and disappointing orders to disband had confronted him with difficult problems of keeping up morale and solving the logistical arrangments for the long march home.

Andrew Jackson passed this, his first major test as a commander, with the highest marks. He was becoming a soldier.

Now he was facing his first real war.

He did not wait.

John Coffee was dispatched south with the cavalry.

When the troops assembled at Fayetteville on the banks of the Elk River, not far from the Alabama border, on October 7, 1813, they could see the erect, spare figure of Old Hickory, with his left arm in a sling, riding about the camp.

Coffee's cavalry was some fifty miles south on the Tennessee River.

On this same day on the continent of Europe, the Duke of Wellington led his Peninsular Army out of Spain into France on the trail of Napoleon. In command of the Iron Duke's military police was his brother-in-law, Major General Sir Edward Pakenham.

It was a name that Jackson had never heard but would know well a little over a year hence.

Four days later, Old Hickory moved his troops out in a forced march to the aid of Coffee, whose cavalry was reported to be in danger. The report was false, but Jackson had moved his men thirty-two miles in nine hours.

His combined forces then put up their main base, Fort Deposit, before plunging deep into Alabama.

In entering the warring Creek country, Jackson was facing their seven-eights white-blooded fighting chief, Red Eagle, whose English name was William Weatherford. He also was in a country where parts of the Creek nation were friendly, as were the Cherokees and Choctaws. It was going to be a mixed-up fight.

But Red Eagle and his Creeks must be punished for the Fort Mims massacre.

Pushing his column through forest and over wild mountain country, Jackson reached the banks of the Coosa River, where he put the soldiers to work on his advanced base, which he named Fort Strother.

While resting there he learned that 200 of Red Eagle's warriors were camped at Tallushatchee some thirteen miles farther on.

Jackson did not wait.

He immediately sent forward John Coffee with 1000 men, one of whom was the later-famous Davy Crockett.

On November 3, 1813, the Creek warriors were surrounded and annihilated.

But Jackson did not have long to savor the victory when a friendly Creek entered his headquarters with a deer tail, the sign of peace, in his hair. He said that Red Eagle was preparing to attack the Creeks, who were for the Americans in Talladega, with a thousand braves.

Again Jackson did not wait.

Although suffering from dysentery, he led his men across the Coosa and through the trackless forest toward Talladega, thirty miles away. By sundown the column was six miles from the town.

While his men slept on their arms, the suffering Jackson spent the night listening to his scouts, who had been sent forward to determine the positions of Red Eagle's warriors and the besieged villagers.

He marched out the troops at dawn to form a huge crescent with two companies of mounted soldiers in the center to act as bait. These cavalrymen rode slowly toward the town where friendly Indians indicated danger off to one flank. The horsemen turned just as Red Eagle's braves opened fire and made for them. The ruse had worked. But the infantry could not contain the surrounded warriors, who broke out of one side of the line and fled.

Seven hundred escaped, leaving 300 dead.

Jackson lost fifteen men in this battle of November 9.

Red Eagle had suffered two severe reverses, and if Old Hickory and his troops had adequate supplies, they might have moved forward and ended the campaign. But it was not to be. Jackson led his men back to Fort Strother, where they were to face two other deadly enemies: starvation and desertion.

6

Horseshoe Bend

STARVATION WAS THE MOST IMMEDIATE THREAT TO THE small army, for when Jackson led his men into Fort Strother, they found the quartermaster's cupboards bare of food.

The troops were respectful but hungry. They wanted to march back to Tennessee to full meals. After that they could return to deal with Red Eagle and his braves.

Finally, after one attempt at desertion by hungry militiamen, Jackson issued a general order on November 13, 1813: "If supplies do not arrive in two days we march back together."

Two days stretched into four days with no food.

On November 17 the columns began to march for home. But twelve miles out from the fort they met a supply train with flour and beef cattle. After a grand feast, the general ordered the troops back to Fort Strother.

With much grumbling, the ranks were formed and one company marched off, but in the wrong direction—toward Tennessee. Others started to follow.

Reacting quickly, Old Hickory blocked their path and then rode into the midst of his men. He seized a musket, and with his left arm still in a sling, laid the piece across his horse's neck, threatening to shoot the first man to disobey him.

Finally the troops marched back to the fort.

But the troubles had not ended. With the enlistment time of two of the militia brigades running out, they were marched north to home.

At one time Jackson's force totalled but 130 men.

Then Governor Blount of Tennessee threw in the towel, recommending Fort Strother be evacuated and the troops retreat to Tennessee.

This was too much for Old Hickory. With scorching pen he wrote Blount:

> Arouse from yr. lethargy—despite fawning smiles or snarling frown—with energy exercise yr. functions—the campaign must rapidly progress or . . . yr. country ruined. Call out the full quota—execute the orders of the Secy of War, arrest the officer who omits his duty. . . . and let popularity perish for the present. . . . Save Mobile—save the Territory—save yr. frontier from becoming drenched in blood. . . . What retrograde under these circumstances? I will perish first.

At this critical moment 800 new recruits marched in.

Jackson again seized the moment. Almost before they knew what was happening, the fledgling soldiers were on the move again—into Creek country. On January 18, 1814, they were camped on the old Talladega battlefield on their way to Red Eagle's main stronghold at the Horseshoe Bend of the Tallapoosa River known as Tohopeka.

On January 21 the troops slept on the banks of Emuckfaw Creek, just three miles from the Horseshoe Bend.

But then things began to become unstuck. Before dawn the Indians attacked. When they were thrown back, Coffee took half the force toward the fortified Creek position at Tohopeka. He found it too strong for Jackson's force to attempt.

After some charges and countercharges, the Creeks were driven off and the painful march back to Fort Strother began.

When the troops reached Enotachopco Creek on the day following the battle, Jackson had them bivouac for the night. He arranged his men so that in case of attack, he could ambush the Indians.

But good plans can go amiss, and these did.

When the warriors struck, Jackson's rearguard folded and fled into the midst of his center, so the whole mass was driven into the cold waters of the Creek, waiting for the scalping knives to do their work.

But the superhuman efforts of William Carroll and John Coffee, under the direction of the cursing and swearing Jackson, held the line. Old Hickory was everywhere.

> In showers of balls he was seen performing the duties of subordinate officers, rallying the alarmed, and inspiriting them by his example. . . . Cowards forgot their panic . . . and the brave would have formed round his body a rampart of their own.

Still Red Eagle's fortress remained intact.

So Jackson would have to try again.

When some 2000 troops faced the log-fronted bastions of the Creeks at the Horseshoe Bend of the Tallapoosa at first light on March 27, 1814, the long war reached its climax.

Bolstered by substantial reinforcements, most notably the Thirty-Ninth U.S. Infantry Regiment, Old Hickory marched south from Fort Strother determined to end the conflict.

He faced a formidable task.

The great bend of the Tallapoosa circled the Creek fortress on three sides, while a strong log barricade pierced by firing ports and manned by 800 warriors barred the way across the isthmus on the land approach.

The Indians had drawn up their canoes on the shore facing the great bend as a means of escape. Their women and children were huddled in the village while their braves manned the barricades.

Jackson sent Coffee with his cavalry to outpost the far bank and seal off the fortress from that side.

Fronting the log-bastion he placed his advance guard with the regular troops of the Thirty-Ninth Infantry in their immediate rear. To their right, his artillery was emplaced on a small hill.

His headquarters and command post, along with the train, were in the rear of the regulars, while the militia units were located still farther back as reserves.

In his general orders Jackson warned, "Any officer or soldier who flies before the enemy without being compelled to do so by superior force . . . shall suffer death."

First action in the coming battle came when Coffee's Cherokee scouts swam the river to the hostile shore to capture the Creek canoes.

The American artillery opened at 10:30 without doing much damage. The six-pound balls sunk into the soft pine logs of the bastion, while the Creek sharpshooters brought telling fire on the artillerymen.

Before noon Jackson held up the action to allow the Indian women and children to be carried across the river and out of harm's way.

At 12:30 the long roll of the drums sent the infantry dashing forward in a charge upon the works. Major Montgomery of the Thirty-Ninth Infantry was the first to scale the barricade, but in an instant he fell back dead.

He was followed by Ensign Sam Houston of his regiment, who leapt over the logs waving his sword and disappeared into the smoke of the battle inside the stockade.

After the bastion was overrun by the Americans, the battle splintered into scores of separate, vicious fights across the wide interior of the fortress.

Houston, who would gain his greatest fame in Texas, wrote, "Arrows, and spears, and balls were flying, swords and tomahawks gleaming in the sun."

Amid the chaos of the battle moved the fighting priests, chanting and dancing their ways through the carnage.

Once Jackson offered peace for surrender. But he got no takers.

The battle went on.

Finally, the killing was over.

More than 500 warriors were slain inside the fortress, with another 200 killed along the river.

The Americans suffered forty-nine killed and 157 wounded.

The power of the Creeks had been broken.

But Red Eagle was not among the slain or wounded.

Later he appeared at Jackson's headquarters, alone and unarmed, to give himself up. But the general let him go free with a handshake.

Old Hickory's return to Nashville was a triumph for the first victorious general of the war. He was commissioned a brigadier general in the United States Army.

Then on May 28, 1814, Jackson was promoted to major general to command the Seventh Military District, including Tennessee, Louisiana and the Mississippi Territory.

Fate now was setting the stage for the greatest challenge this self-taught soldier ever would face.

Part III

I think I have escaped America, and shall consider myself vastly fortunate to have been spared such a service.
—Major General Sir Edward Pakenham,
June 1814.

7

Knockout Blows

FOUR DAYS AFTER JACKSON'S VICTORY AT HORSESHOE BEND, another general was tasting the bitter dregs of defeat.

On March 31, 1814, in faraway Paris, the conquering columns of Prussia, Russia and Austria marched into the City of Light. The following day Napoleon, support crumbling on all sides, abdicated his throne for the principality of Elba.

The war for Europe was over, or so the Allied powers thought.

The triumphant British Army that had crossed into the south of France from Spain under Wellington now would be ready to force the surrender of the United States to England's will.

But no time should be lost for the grand assault.

It would be a gigantic operation, consisting of a series of

multiple invasions: from Canada on the north, from the Atlantic against the American coasts, and from the south into Louisiana.

The city of New Orleans would be one of the prime targets.

These plans were outlined for the Iron Duke by Frederick, Duke of York, brother of the Prince Regent and commander in chief of the British Army, in a letter dated April 14.

Four powerful divisions would be taken from Wellington's successful peninsular army for service in America. The total number of troops to be embarked would be 16,300 officers and men. These were the finest professional soldiers Britain could muster.

In his letter, His Royal Highness advised Wellington that he desired the duke's brother-in-law, Sir Edward Pakenham, "should be employed upon this service, provided an acceptable command could be procured for him."

The thrusts against the American Atlantic seaboard would be under the command of Admiral Sir Alexander Cochrane, commander in chief of British naval forces on the American station.

They would not be long in coming.

Early in the summer of 1814, Cochrane had ravaged the New England coast, burning the town of Eastport, Maine, capturing Nantucket, and raiding Cape Cod and Long Island Sound.

A salt-stained veteran of the Napoleonic Wars at sea, he was a rather heavy featured man, not too concerned where the painful wounds of war might fall.

He already had made up his mind where his major blows would strike, in keeping with the general directive issued to his blockading squadrons: "Destroy and lay waste such towns and cities upon the coast as you may find assailable. Spare merely the lives of the unarmed inhabitants of the United States."

8

Royal Arson

THE CUTTING EDGE OF COCHRANE'S ATTACK ON AMERICA'S Atlantic coast would be one of Wellington's crack divisions commanded by Major General Robert Ross, including the Fourth, Forty-Fourth and Eighty-Fifth Regiments. With their artillery and other supporting troops, these regiments totalled more than 3000 men.

Sailing under armed convoy from the south of France in early June, Ross would pause at Bermuda to be reinforced by the Twenty-First Regiment, the Royal North Britain Fusiliers. The next port would be Tangier Island in the middle of Chesapeake Bay, where they joined Cochrane's fleet on August 15 to prepare for invasion. The admiral added his marines to give Ross more than 4000 men.

In spite of his fears, Pakenham had not sailed for America, and remained in France as Wellington's adjutant general.

Four days later Ross put his men ashore on the western banks of the Patuxent River near the village of Benedict, fifty road miles from Washington, the capital of the United States.

Marching his veterans north, Ross halted his columns on August 22 near Upper Marlborough. He now was but sixteen miles east of Washington and thirty miles south of the great port of Baltimore.

At this point Commodore Joshua Barney of the United States Navy, was forced to burn his small flotilla of gunboats and deploy his seamen in defensive positions to cover the approaches to the capital.

Now General Ross would have to make a decision. Which would he attack: Washington or Baltimore?

He chose Washington.

The almost defenseless city was in a state of general confusion.

President James Madison was busy calling for help from the neighboring states while Secretary of State James Monroe was galloping over the countryside playing scout. The secretaries of war, navy and treasury were equally ineffective in the crisis.

The military commander, Brigadier General Winder, was just as helpless, claiming he had "accepted the command without means and without time to create them." He found the district "without magazines of provision or forage, without transport, tools or implements, without a commissariat or efficient quartermaster's department, without a general staff, and finally without troops."

In spite of it all, there were roughly 7000 American troops in the area. However, only Commodore Barney seemed to know what he was doing. He took a position in advance of Bladensburg with his naval guns, where he cleared the road of British infantry twice before he had been flanked and wounded.

A British lieutenant with the Eighty-Fifth Light Infantry, George Robert Gleig, admired that the sailors did not only "serve their guns with a quickness and precision which astonished their assailants, but they stood till some of them were actually bayoneted, with fuzes in their hands."

His men becoming exhausted in the Potomac Valley heat, Ross rested them for two hours and then personally led the advance into Washington's dark and deserted streets. He had suffered sixty-four killed and 185 wounded.

In his advance he had the company of Admiral George Cockburn, second in command to Admiral Cochrane.

When they reached the center of the city, musket fire brought down Ross's horse for the second time. It was August 24, 1814, a day of disgrace for both nations.

The two British commanders then proceeded to direct the burning of the Capitol, the White House, the National Archives, the Treasury, the War Office, all the public buildings, and, of course, all the military and naval installations and stores their troops could reach.

It was a savage and brutal act, to be justified by the British high command as fit retaliation for the American burning of York, capital of Upper Canada, in April 1813.

But not all British officers viewed it that way. Captain Harry Smith, later a major on Ross's staff, disapproved:

> We entered Washington for the barbarous purpose of destroying the city. Admiral Cockburn would have burnt the whole, but Ross would only consent to the burning of public buildings. I had no objection to burn arsenals, dockyards, frigates building, stores, barracks, etc., but well do I recollect that, fresh from the Duke's humane warfare in the South of France, we were horrified at the order to burn the elegant Houses of Parliament and the President's house.

The following day, while the flames still were burning in the devastated city, the skies darkened at noon. Lightning flashed in fury over the wondering invaders as hurricane-force winds of a Maryland thundergust drove drenching rains through the deserted streets.

Ross decided to pull out and marched his troops away on the long journey back to the ships.

He left the government of the United States in disarray.

9

Immortal Banner

WITH THEIR FIRST SMASH AT THE YANKEES, COCHRANE, Cockburn and Ross readied their second punch.

It would be a much heavier naval blow aimed at Baltimore.

It would be delivered with staggering force.

There would be fifty-six ships sailing up Chesapeake Bay to assault Baltimore from the Patapsco River, led by four line-of-battle ships: the flagship *Tonnant* with eighty guns, and the seventy-fours *Albion, Dragon* and *Royal Oak*.

Following them would be the frigates, sloops-of-war, bomb vessels, rocket ships, gun brigs, mortar boats, tenders and finally the transports packed with Ross's 4,200 soldiers and marines.

While his aides were readying this mighty force, Admiral Cochrane already was planning for the great invasion in the south—objective: New Orleans.

To incite the Indians, Spanish and French in Louisiana to rise against the Americans, he had sent Lieutenant Colonel Edward Nicholls to the Gulf of Mexico with a contingent of marines aboard the ships *Hermes* and *Carron.*

It was this activity that led General Andrew Jackson, after he had dictated peace terms to the Creek Indians, to march his Third U.S. Infantry to Mobile, Alabama, to forestall the British plans.

But Baltimore would come first.

Dispatch riders pounded north to Baltimore with the news that "twenty-six sail had passed Point Lookout at the mouth of the Potomac, Monday, September 5." Thirty more war vessels had been counted "beating up" the Chesapeake by four o'clock on the afternoon of Thursday the 8th. The peril to the city was growing hourly.

Defense of Baltimore had been entrusted to a sixty-two-year-old veteran of the Revolutionary War, Major General Samuel Smith of the Maryland Militia. He began fortifying the approaches to the city as soon as the danger of invasion became apparent.

He would prove to be a very tough commander. He would have a very tough job.

Baltimore, at this time the fourth-largest city in the United States, a great seaport, and home to many of the privateers devastating the British merchant marine, lay at the head of the vast Chesapeake Bay with its miles of undefended shoreline.

At the entrance to its harbor, it was protected by Fort McHenry, a star-shaped masonry-walled stronghold armed with old cannon too short-ranged to provide adequate protection against any determined seaborne assault.

Yet McHenry would prove to be the star of the show that was to transpire around her in the following few days.

She also would fly the largest United States flag in the nation, some thirty-six-feet long and twenty-nine-feet high.

This would become the Immortal Banner of American history.

But the fighting would not start here.

It would begin on Monday, September 12, after Vice Admiral Cochrane silently landed General Ross with his soldiers, marines and sailors, now swollen in numbers to more than 5000 officers and men.

The landing had been conducted with great skill, beginning in the dark hours after three o'clock in the morning off the protecting headland of North Point. Once ashore, the troops began a pleasant fourteen-mile march to Baltimore through the autumn woodland.

It all was so easy that General Ross and Admiral Cockburn paused to have a leisurely breakfast at a captured farmhouse.

After that things did not go so well.

When the advance resumed after noon, Ross mounted his white horse to ride at the head of his main column. There came a scattering of shots from the woodland in front. But when the advance guard did not settle the matter, Ross rode forward to see why.

He learned fast enough.

Two shots rang out and he fell, fatally wounded. The pleasant march had ended.

By the time Colonel Francis Brooke took over command, he found his troops embroiled in battle with Sam Smith's forward regiments. After heavy action he pushed them back and his army bivouaced on the eastern outskirts of Baltimore to prepare for the final assault.

Meanwhile the British fleet had spent Monday's hours moving their mortar-bomb and rocket vessels slowly upriver to within range of Fort McHenry. The naval assault would come tomorrow.

A rainstorm came roaring over Maryland after midnight to mark the start of the second day of battle.

The battle opened a little after sunrise (which came at 5:46 A.M.) when the first bomb ship fired its thirteen-inch powder-filled shell. It went up almost out of sight, arced over and started down faster and ever faster to drop its 200 pounds of explosive. It blew up harmlessly behind McHenry on Whetstone Point.

It was the first of many shells, for the bombardment

would go on for twenty-five hours, with hardly a pause throughout Tuesday, to finally end on Wednesday morning at 7 o'clock.

With McHenry and its batteries growling their replies, the roar of noise over the fort and harbor was tremendous.

Meanwhile, Colonel Brooke was searching for a weak-spot in General Sam Smith's lines about the city, but he couldn't find a way of attack that would not be too costly to attempt.

A final effort was made by the fleet and the army after midnight, but it was aborted with no gain.

Finally at 3 A.M. on Wednesday, hidden in the darkness behind a shield of flaming campfires, the retreat began down the long road to the boats. The ships before McHenry set sail down river about nine o'clock to pick up the troops.

The battle for Baltimore was over.

For Baltimorean Francis Scott Key, who had watched the attack while an unwilling cartel passenger on a British ship, McHenry's great flag flying over the embattled fort would inspire the writing of the young nation's national anthem.

It truly was an Immortal Banner.

10

Fumbler's Fiasco

THE BLOW FROM THE NORTH WOULD BE THE HARDEST OF all. It would be delivered under the direction of Lieutenant General Sir George Prevost, a distinguished soldier of the king. He was not only governor of all Canada but also commander in chief of the armed services.

In June 1814, he was instructed by British Colonial Secretary Lord Bathurst to prepare for the invasion of the United States. His forces would advance from Canada down the Lake Champlain-Hudson River line to New York City, thus splitting off the New England states, which were opposed to the war, from the rest of the former colonies.

To do this job he would receive two of the three victorious divisions of Lord Wellington's army destined for North America to whip United States forces and bring the War of 1812 to an end.

The other Peninsular division under General Robert Ross would go to Vice Admiral Cochrane for the attacks on Washington and Baltimore.

These powerful forces would give Sir George 11,000 men to make his devastating descent upon the Americans.

But Sir George also was a very cautious man.

Would he be up to conducting the bold, slashing attack from the north that Britain's present situation in the unfortunate war demanded?

Past performances suggested otherwise.

At the beginning of the war, it had been the fast moving, hard-hitting General Isaac Brock who had carried the war to the Americans in Upper Canada before his death in action at Queenstown Heights near Niagara. Prevost, charged with holding the long river lines of Lower Canada against invasion, had preferred the defensive.

In this he had done a superb job, throwing back a series of inept American attacks without suffering severe losses.

However, prior to the Battle of Lake Erie on September 10, 1813, he had urged his naval commander, Captain Robert Barclay, to seek out and destroy the American squadron under Captain Oliver Hazard Perry, before the British flotilla was prepared for action. The British were defeated in a long and bloody fight.

In September 1814, with Admiral Cochrane burning Washington and attacking Baltimore, Sir George was in command of a superb army of 11,000 men, most of whom were battle-tried veterans who had served under Wellington. They were across the border on the west shore of Lake Champlain, having advanced south from Montreal.

Wellington's veterans were having no trouble with American frontier troops. They brushed them aside with contempt, without pausing to deploy before their columns pressed on toward their objective, the American base at Plattsburg, New York, close to the border on the west side of Lake Champlain.

Here with but four infantry and three artillery companies totalling 1,500 soldiers, Brigadier General Alexander Macomb prepared to bar the way of the invader.

Even though he had been strengthened by units of the New York State militia, Macomb would be facing three-to-one odds.

It looked like a sure thing for the British.

But Sir George didn't think so.

He must have his naval support from the lake—or so he thought.

To this end he kept badgering Captain George Downie of the Royal Navy to sail against the American flotilla lying at anchor in Plattsburg Bay, before his ships were ready for battle.

Downie, who had arrived to take command on September 2, after the troops were well on their way south, needed time to prepare his fleet. But Sir George wouldn't give him time.

Finally Captain Downie gave in to his superior and stood down the lake in support of the land force.

But here again the cautious general saw his overwhelming force operating in support of the navy. It was going to be a mixed-up job.

To the south Macomb's troops burned the bridges across the Saranac River as Prevost's veterans entered the north side of the town. They then moved into their entrenchments, where their cannon looked down over Plattsburg and out toward the bay where Thomas Macdonough's squadron of sixteen vessels lay at anchor.

Macdonough's mission was simple: keep the British fleet from bombarding the American positions.

His battle plan was even simpler.

His four major vessels would fire broadsides from one side during the initial stages of the fight and then swing their undamaged sides toward the enemy and fire more broadsides at the foe. The mooring lines were run out to facilitate this turning movement.

Meanwhile his smaller gunboats would harrass the enemy wherever they could.

On the morning of September 11, the British fleet came down the lake firing their signal guns so Prevost could launch his land assault. But he did nothing for a time.

Macdonough waited for the enemy to approach, only to see the wind die away, forcing the British to come to anchor as close to the Americans as they could get.

Then the slugging match began.

In the first fifteen minutes Captain Downie was slain in the fierce melee.

After two hours the American flagship, the twenty-six-gun *Saratoga*, forced the larger British flagship, the thirty-six-gun *Confiance,* to strike her colors. Most of the invading fleet was near sinking.

Macdonough had the victory.

Ashore, Sir George's veteran troops became lost, failed to cross the river, and were bugled into retreat without accomplishing much of anything.

Back in Canada their general-in-chief would be called home to face a court-martial but would die before it could be convened.

Another British thrust at her former colonies had failed.

11

Fluttering Dove

WHILE BRITISH EFFORTS TO BRING AMERICA TO ITS KNEES were failing on the various battlefronts, halting and acrimonious gestures toward a peaceful settlement of the war were being made by both sides in talks in the ancient city of Ghent in North Belgium.

Beginning on August 8, 1814, the two sides began backing their way towards some kind of consensus on how to end the war, which was growing increasingly unpopular in both countries.

The American delegation, led by Ambassador to Russia John Quincy Adams, included Speaker of the House of Representatives Henry Clay, former Secretary of the Treasury Albert Gallatin, Delaware Senator James Bayard, and Johnathan Russell, charge d'affaires in London. They all were able men, but they were torn by both political and personal differences.

45

The British commissioners were a mixed bag headed by Vice Admiral Lord Gambier, commander of the Channel Fleet from 1808 to 1811, resplendent in his gold-laced uniform. He was assisted by London lawyer William Adams, Under Secretary for War Henry Gouldburn, and Anthony St. John Baker. Baker was a former attaché to the British Embassy in Washington, where he had made himself exceedingly disliked. He served as secretary.

The Americans were dealing from an increasingly deteriorating position while the British taking heart from Cockburn's advance on Washington, presented ever-harsher demands on the part of their government. The British also were counting on what was deemed the almost sure success of Prevost's thrust southward at New York coupled with the following expedition against New Orleans.

These expectations were reflected in stiff terms delivered by British foreign secretary Lord Castlereagh, who stopped over in Ghent on August 19 to brief his delegation while en route to the Congress of Vienna. In America Cockburn and Ross were marching their troops toward Washington.

When the Americans were told the terms, they scarcely could believe them.

A buffer Indian state would be created between the United States and Canada; control of the Great Lakes would pass to the hands of the British, who would retain their rights to navigation of the Mississippi River with access from Lake Superior; no American war vessels or forts would be allowed along the lakes; and part of Maine would be ceded to allow a direct road from Quebec to Halifax.

There was no mention at all of the impressment of seamen on the high seas, which had been the reason for the American declaration of war in the first place.

Adams and his delegation could not accept these terms. They delivered their refusal four days later.

The day before in America, the city of Washington had been burned.

Part IV

*Before one month the British and Spanish
forces expect to be in Possession of Mobile
and all the surrounding country. There will
be bloody noses before this happens.*
—Jackson to his ward, Robert Butler,
on August 27, 1814

12

On Mobile Bay

WHEN JACKSON RODE INTO MOBILE AT THE HEAD OF THE U.S. Third Infantry Regiment on August 22, 1814, he already had his eyes on Pensacola in Spanish Florida, where the British had landed troops while Old Hickory had been engaged in completing a treaty with the Creek Indians at Fort Jackson in Alabama Territory. It was a treaty that would break the power of the Creek tribe forever.

Here he was to learn that, as he wrote to his ward Robert Butler:

His B.M. ships *Hermes, Carron* and *Sophy* has arrived at Pensacola . . . and taken possession. The *Orpheus* is expected in a few days with 14 sail of the line and *Transports* has arrived at Barmuda, with 25,000 of Lord Wellingtons army &c. &c., before one month the British and Spanish forces expect to be in Possession of Mobile and all the surrounding country. There will be bloody noses before this happens.

To back up his threat, he sped Major William Lawrence with 160 men to abandoned Fort Bowyer at the tip of the sand spit commanding the gulf entrance to Mobile Bay. Lawrence prepared the works for war.

Lawrence threw himself into the task in a frenzy matched only by that of his commander, Jackson, at Mobile itself.

Ever so slowly, more forces for the defense of the United States' southern coasts were being assembled. In these efforts they were to be granted some surcease by the slowness of the British. For it would not be until September 13 that Sir William Percy of the Royal Navy would land Colonel Edward Nicholls's marines and Indians at the base of the spit on which Fort Bowyer stood.

Shortly thereafter, *Sophie, Hermes, Carron* and *Childers*, would stand into the channel to prepare for the business at hand.

Major Lawrence, watching these preparations for attack, put down his glass to call Lieutenant Roy to him. He would have to have help to hold the fort, and Roy would go to Mobile and get it.

While Roy's small craft was beating its way through heavy seas against a headwind from the north, a strange thing was happening at Mobile.

With that sixth sense that marked much of his life, Jackson had decided to run down to his guardian fort to check things out. Leaving at 10 p.m. with a heavy wind astern, his schooner was racing through the seas when Roy's craft was sighted coming north.

Learning of the call for help, Jackson put about, but because of the headwind he did not reach Mobile until nightfall. When there he lost no time in putting Captain Laval's company of the Third Infantry aboard a boat for Fort Bowyer.

But the reinforcement effort was in vain, for Laval returned to Mobile on September 16 with news that while still four miles from the fort, the relieving party had seen the British ships bombarding the fort while marines and Indians attacked along the sand spit. The British flagship had been disabled by Bowyer's fire, but that night, when an explosion rocked the fort, Captain Laval, declaring her magazine destroyed, turned back for Mobile.

He was wrong, however.

Beaten off by the fort's fire, Percy had been forced to blow up the disabled *Hermes*. The shore party retreated and Major Lawrence had a victory.

First blood for Jackson.

13

A New Enemy

OLD HICKORY HAD ONE MORE PIECE OF UNFINISHED BUSI-
ness—the town of Pensacola in Spanish Florida,
some sixty miles to the east.

Although Spain officially was neutral, British ships and
marines had been seen in the harbor and in the antiquated
forts that guarded access from the gulf.

He would bag these English forces.

"The safety of this section of the union depends upon it
. . . and Pensacola has assumed the character of British
Territory," he advised Secretary of War James Monroe
before he marched his troops out of their camps on the
Alabama River on November 2, 1814.

It was quite an army—3000 strong.

Seven hundred were Regulars, the Third and Forty-
Fourth Infantry Regiments.

Eighteen hundred were Tennessee cavalrymen, each with his own horse and rifle. They were led by Jackson's old comrade-in-arms, Brigadier General John Coffee, firm of jaw and will.

The expedition would be a tough one for the British and Spanish to handle.

Nevertheless, when Jackson sent Major Peire of the Forty-fourth forward under a flag of truce on November 5 to "require that the different forts, Barrancas, St. Rose, and St. Michael, should be immediately surrendered to be garrisoned . . . by the United States, until Spain . . . could preserve unimpaired her neutral character," his party was taken under fire.

Anticipating the refusal, Jackson had the army, in full view of the seven Royal Navy men-of-war in the harbor and the Spanish soldiers in the fort, go into camp along the highway leading into Pensacola from the west. If there was to be a fight, he would attack from there.

Or so the British and the Spanish thought.

But during the black hours before dawn, Old Hickory marched his infantry noiselessly around the town while Coffee's horse soldiers made plenty of racket mounting an attack from the old encampment.

When the main assault went in from the east, it took both the Spanish in the forts and the British on the ships by complete surprise.

Following some house-to-house fighting in the old city and the repulse of a British attempt from their ships, a shaken Spanish commandant was forced to surrender.

He delayed long enough, however, so that Jackson would not be able to proceed against Barrancas, some seven miles away, without reorganizing his troops.

Just as they were preparing to move out at about three o'clock the following morning, a sharp blast rocked the ground under their feet.

The British had blown up the fort and put to sea with some of the Spanish troops.

Jackson had been cheated.

But maybe he had been lured away from defending Mobile.

Three and one-half days of forced marches brought them all back to where they had started, and Mobile was safe.

And Jackson had another victory.

14

The Pirates

JUST PRIOR TO THE ATTACK ON FORT BOWYER, A BRITISH sloop-of-war had put in to Grand Terre Island at the mouth of Barataria Bay in the Mississippi delta, just west of the great river, on a strange mission.

The British sought the services of renowned pirate Jean Laffite on the side of England in her war with the United States.

Lafitte heard the British captain out. He promised to consider the offer of a captaincy in the Royal Navy, a reward of $30,000, lands and other spoils of war, and then asked him to return in two weeks for his answer.

When the British captain returned after the repulse of the attack on Fort Bowyer, he found Grand Terre deserted and Lafitte gone.

What he could not know was that in the meantime

Governor of Louisiana William Claiborne had sent an armed expedition to clean out the pirates' nest, only to be met with no resistance and protestations of loyalty to the United States. Jean and his brother Pierre Lafitte had escaped.

Their eldest brother, Dominique Youx, remaining in command of the 500 men on the island, was taken in chains along with eighty of the pirates and thrown into prison.

Then began an involved campaign to use the pirates in defense of the city.

Even the governor was now in favor of this action.

But Jackson was not impressed.

He recommended to Claiborne that he arrest them all, and labeled Laffite and his men "this hellish Banditti."

But even Old Hickory was to change his mind under most unusual circumstances.

15

The British

WHILE JACKSON WAS MARCHING AGAINST PENSACOLA, the British were concentrating the most powerful army and navy expedition ever sent against the southern coasts of the United States.

The Royal Navy fleets would be under command of the most skillful, experienced, and ruthless admirals on the American station: Admiral Sir Alexander Cochrane, Rear Admiral Sir George Cockburn, and Rear Admiral Sir Pulteney Malcolm. Rear Admiral Sir Edward Codrington served as chief of staff for Cochrane.

This naval high command had long experience in American waters. Under their command were roughly 10,000 seamen and marines.

The British Army command would join their naval counterparts somewhat later.

When all the land forces were joined, they would number more than 8000 battle-hardened veterans of Wellington's campaigns in Spain against the French.

Commander in chief would be Major General Sir Edward Pakenham, brother-in-law and adjutant general for Wellington.

Although he had hoped to "escape America," he had loyally accepted the command as "I cannot resist a National call or the feelings of my Personal Duty."

The command came to Pakenham after a series of battlefield misfortunes and a high government decision.

When the New Orleans attack had been first decided upon, it was to be led by Lieutenant General Sir John Hope. However, when he was wounded before Bayonne in Wellington's advance on southwest France, it was offered to Lieutenant General Sir Rowland Hill, the Iron Duke's second-in-command. But then London had a change of mind and decided that, after all, the hard-driving General Robert Ross was the man for the job.

Ross's death in the advance on Baltimore settled that, and the choice came to Pakenham, like it or not.

Ned Pakenham was a veteran soldier who had served as an officer in the British Army since the age of sixteen. He saw action against the French in Ireland in 1798; in Canada in 1801; in the West Indies in 1803; Copenhagen in 1808; Martinique in 1809; then with Wellington in the Peninsular Campaign from 1809 until the final victory.

On receiving his orders in October 1814, the thirty-five-year-old bachelor wrote his mother: "The Affairs in America have gone ill—staff officers have become necessary, and I have been called on by the Ministers to proceed to the other side of the Atlantic. I confess to you that there is nothing that makes this employment desireable. . . ."

He sailed from Spithead off Portsmouth with his staff aboard the frigate *Statira* on November 1, 1814, under secret orders to a rendezvous with the rest of his army at Negril Bay on the west coast of Jamaica ninety miles south of Cuba.

With him in *Statira* were Major General Samuel Gibbs, who would command one of the brigades of the army; Major Harry Smith, assistant adjutant general; Lieutenant Colonel John Fox Burgoyne, chief engineer officer and the illegitimate son of General John Burgoyne, who had surrendered at Saratoga in the Revolution; Lieutenant Colonel Alexander Dickson, chief artillery officer with a wide reputation as the leading gunnery officer in the British Army; and, finally, Surgeon General John Robb.

The *Statira* would not arrive at the rendezvous at Negril Bay until December 13. There Pakenham found Major General John Lambert waiting with 2000 troops, having sailed from England a week before his commander in chief.

But just as Pakenham had feared, there was no sign of Admiral Cochrane and the bulk of the army under Major General John Keane, which had sailed from Plymouth in September to reinforce Ross's division.

The salty admiral, tired of waiting for Pakenham, had sailed from Negril Bay for the Louisiana coast on November 26 with Keane's troops and the rest of the fleet following on the next day.

Pakenham was now in a state of great apprehension that he would not arrive at the scene of operations before the troops had been put on shore. After a quick conference with Lambert on *Statira,* he left him to continue taking on water and provisions for his troops and sailed in the wake of his absent admiral.

Artillery Commander Colonel Dickson wrote in his journal: "I fear . . . we shall not arrive in time to partake of the operation."

They would get there eventually, but not in time for the opening guns.

When Cochrane and Keane sailed north with the bulk of the troops, they would be taking with them some of the finest soldiers in the British Army.

There would be the Ninety-Third Regiment (Argyll and Sutherland Highlanders), six companies of the Ninety-

Fifth (Rifle Brigade), a squadron of the Fourteenth Light Dragoons, the Fifth West India Regiment, a company of artillery, a company of engineers, and a detachment of the Rocket Brigade.

These troops were in addition to those of Colonel Brooke's brigade from the Chesapeake Bay campaign: the Eighty-Fifth (King's Shropshire Light Infantry), the Fourth (The King's Own), the Twenty-First (Royal Scots Fusiliers) and the Forty-Fourth (Essex Regiment) plus sappers, miners and artillerymen.

Even though their commanding general was in a nervous and uncertain state of mind, the British were bringing overwhelming force against the self-taught general and his motley crew of regulars, militia, pirates, frontiersmen, free negroes and Indians.

16

The Americans

WHILE HIS OPPONENT WAS STRIVING TO GAIN HIS RIGHT-ful place at the head of his army, Old Hickory kept guard over Mobile, convinced that the British would strike there first to gain a base from which to launch their overland attack on New Orleans.

With him were his Regulars of the Third and Forty-fourth Infantry regiments, and the militia, which had captured Pensacola.

Brigadier General John Coffee had been dispatched to Baton Rouge to wait and see which way the cat was going to jump. He had taken his cavalry with him.

Along with Coffee, Brigadier General William Carroll, the other long-trusted member of the high command, was supposed to be marching down from Tennessee with a large contingent of volunteers.

Actually, Carroll, in disobedience of Jackson's orders, was not marching at all. He and his 3000 Tennessee militiamen were floating down the Cumberland River in flatboats en route to the Ohio and the Mississippi Rivers. The handsome Tennessean had estimated that the river voyage, although longer, would in fact take less time.

So he shoved off with his staff and troops from Nashville hoping he would be proven right.

If not?

Well, everyone in the assembling army was familiar with the short temper of their commander in chief.

There was the high command of the land forces of the United States in the coming battle. There would be other generals, but these three, Jackson, Coffee and Carroll, would be the core of command.

There was not a professional soldier among them. All their battle skills were honed in the Indian Wars or perfected by their own reading and study.

Jackson's small flotilla of naval vessels was under the command of two professional U.S. Navy officers who were to render him excellent service: Commodore Daniel Patterson and Lieutenant Thomas ap Catesby Jones.

Nevertheless, the British Army generals in their scarlet and gold, and the Royal Navy admirals in their blue uniforms trimmed with gold lace, would have been bemused by this odd assortment of commanders preparing to take their motley collection of troops into battle against the most professional army and navy in the world.

In his order of battle, Jackson would count the Seventh and Forty-fourth Regular Infantry Regiments, General Coffee's 1250 cavalrymen, General Carroll's 3000 Tennessee militiamen, General John Thomas and his 2300 Kentucky volunteers, Thomas Hinds and 150 Mississippi dragoons, several small regiments of Louisiana militia, plus the special volunteer battalions from the City of New Orleans and the Pirates of Jean Lafitte and his brother, Dominique Youx.

The totals mounted up in numbers, but the trouble was that not all of these troops were in the arena of action.

Coffee was at Baton Rouge; Carroll was coming down the Mississippi in flatboats followed by Thomas and John Adair with their Kentuckians; many of the troops were on outpost duty, and Jackson had left a sizable force at Mobile and Fort Bowyer.

Jackson had not yet left Mobile; he was convinced that this was the point of attack.

Finally, on November 22, he yielded to the pleas of Louisiana Governor Claiborne for his presence in New Orleans, and set out for the Queen City of the Mississippi.

He would take twelve days on the way, scouting all the inlets, bays and bayous that might afford a welcoming entry to the British juggernaut that now was somewhere out in the gulf.

Jackson himself was beginning to show the strains of the great stress under which he labored. In addition, the growing pains of his dysentery were beginning to show their presence. They would last throughout the campaign.

He was ready to make his entrance to the city that he had been chosen to defend.

Would he be successful?

Only time and the river would tell.

Part V

Whoever is not for us, is against us.
—General Andrew Jackson to Louisiana
Governor Claiborne, December 1814

17

The Prize

NEW ORLEANS IN 1814 WAS A CITY THAT STILL WAS NOT sure it was comfortable under the American flag.

Little more than a hundred miles from mouth of the Mississippi, which flows past its levees, it already was one of the great ports of the world with the promise of even greater days to come.

Settled by the French in 1718, it rapidly had acquired a style and character unique in the New World. It was French—and French it would remain.

But not officially.

For in 1762 Louis XV made a gift of the "Isle of Orleans" to his cousin, Charles III of Spain.

The French-speaking citizenry were irate, but their protests to the king were not even presented to him.

They were Spanish, and Spanish they would remain—at

least until 1800, when their city was returned to French rule.

This upset the United States, which visualized Napoleon's troops marching through the streets of the largest city on her southern doorstep.

But the Creoles of New Orleans were jubilant. They were French again.

It wouldn't be for long, however, for in 1803 the greatest real estate deal in history would put the Creoles under the stars and stripes. Napoleon sold the huge Louisiana Territory to the United States for about $16,000,000.

The first governor of the territory would be William Claiborne, who had once filled Andrew Jackson's vacated seat in the U.S. Congress in 1797. He would become governor of the state when Louisiana was admitted as the 18th state in the Union in 1812.

Now as he tried to keep control of the many diverse elements in his lively, almost unruly city, faced with the threat of British invasion, he beseeched Jackson to come to New Orleans to direct its defense.

It was then that Old Hickory, not a little annoyed by the constant calls for aid from Claiborne, decided to go to New Orleans.

For the British, the capture of New Orleans held out some intriguing possibilities.

One of them had been set forth by Colonial Secretary Lord Bathurst, who had written to the now-deceased General Robert Ross back on September 6:

> If you shall find in the inhabitants a general and decided disposition to withdraw from their recent connection with the United States, either with the view of establishing themselves as an independent people or of returning under the dominion of the Spanish Crown, you will give them every support in your power; you will furnish them with arms and clothing, and assist in forming and disciplining the several levies, provided you are fully satisfied of their intentions, which will be best evinced by their committing themselves in some act of decided hostility against the United

States. . . . You will discountenance any proposition of the inhabitants to place themselves under the dominion of Great Britain; and you will direct their disposition toward returning under the protection of the Spanish Crown rather than to the attempting to maintain what it will be much more difficult to secure substantially,—their independence as a separate State; and you must give them clearly to understand that Great Britain cannot pledge herself to make the independence of Louisiana, or its restoration to the Spanish Crown, a sine qua non of peace with the United States.

Bathurst also wrote to Admiral Cochrane on the same day setting forth the objectives of the southern expedition:

First to obtain command of the embouchure of the Mississippi, so as to deprive the back settlements of America of their communication with the sea; and, secondly, to occupy some important and valuable possession, by the restoration of which the conditions of peace might be improved, or which we might be entitled to exact the cessation of, as the price of peace.

So the British were playing for big game, indeed!

18

The Problem

RIDING WESTWARD TOWARD NEW ORLEANS, JACKSON PON-
dered the problem of sealing off the many routes of
access into the city both by land and sea. It was going to be
most difficult. To be successful he was going to need all the
help he could get and soon.

In his flag quarters in the mighty eighty-gun ship-of-
the-line *Tonnant*, captured from the French in the Battle of
the Nile in 1798, Admiral Sir Alexander Cochrane was
mulling over the same question but from the mirror point
of view.

Jackson had to defend the city.

Cochrane would attack it with the British Army.

The great delta on which New Orleans sits, sprawls like
a human hand thrust palm down out into the Gulf of
Mexico.

With the city located at the wrist, the right thumb would encompass the two large lakes on the north, Lake Pontchartrain and Lake Borgne. Then moving toward the index finger to the east, there were a multitude of salt and freshwater bayous leading from Lake Borgne and the gulf and on toward the city and the river. The middle finger, pointing southeast, would signify the Father of Waters himself, the Mississippi, which provided a broad water road to the heart of the city. The ring finger to the south would represent Barataria Bay, home of Lafitte and his pirates. Lastly, the little finger to the south and west would cover Bayou La Fourche, offering a difficult but possible approach route.

It was a vast watery world of swamp, gulf and river.

Jackson would have to cover all approaches.

Cochrane only would have to pick one where he could put the troops ashore without a bloody fight—if he could find it.

With his dysentery acting up and his tired mind burdened with the problems of troop concentrations to cover enemy approaches, supply of ammunition and food, construction of obstacles, and plans for battle when and where it should come, Jackson entered a city in complete disarray.

In unadorned uniform and knee-high dragoon boots, his ramrod straight figure wrapped in a blue Spanish cloak, it was his fierce hawklike eyes blazing out from under his small leather cap that most impressed the throng of fearful well-wishers that bade him welcome to New Orleans on December 1, 1814.

Headquarters was set up rapidly at 106 Rue Royale and the business of preparing for the coming assault begun.

Three days before, the main strength of the British fleet, fifty sail, had put out from Jamaica with the bulk of General Keane's division aboard. They were bound for Ship and Cat Islands at the mouth of Lake Borgne, where it joined the gulf.

Jackson was not to be given much time.

19

The Plans

IN HIS HEADQUARTERS IN RUE ROYALE, JACKSON FACED A city that simply would not believe it was under siege. Citizens moved slowly as if the war were far away and would not come closer. If it did, they were certain someone from somewhere would come to their rescue.

Jackson changed all that.

In a series of rapid-fire orders, he began to vitalize the defenses of New Orleans.

Commodore Patterson would station Lieutenant ap Catesby Jones with five gunboats on Lake Borgne along with a schooner, *Seahorse*, and tender, *Alligator*, to cover the sea approaches from the northeast and east. Parties of axmen and engineers would fell trees and erect barriers across the bayous on the east.

The Mississippi would be barred to the invaders by a

strengthened Fort St. Philip some fifty miles below the city. English Turn, where the river makes a great bend just below the city, would see the emplacement of new batteries at old Fort St. Leon, with others put in place at Fort Bourbon across from Fort St. Philip and at Terre aux Boeufs opposite Fort St. Leon.

Parties of militia, engineers and axmen were put to work on barriers to the more unlikely western approaches.

Commodore Patterson would keep the fourteen-gun schooner *Carolina* and the sixteen-gun armed sloop *Louisiana* before New Orleans for use on the river. It would prove to be a most wise decision.

On December 3, Jackson reviewed the New Orleans Volunteer Battalion in the Place d'Armes.

Slowly the spirit of resistance to the invaders began to build.

The next day Old Hickory went down the river on a six-day inspection of the fortifications.

Meanwhile, his opponents, Cochrane and Keane, had been off the West Florida coast seeking Indian assistance in their plans, but with little success.

Before Jackson returned to New Orleans, the *Tonnant* and four other British men-of-war had anchored between Ship Island and the Chandeleur Islands east of New Orleans, where their presence promptly was reported to Commodore Patterson by Lieutenant Jones.

The net was drawing closer.

When Jackson returned to New Orleans, he immediately took off again on a personal inspection of the routes leading into the city from Lakes Borgne and Pontchartrain. More batteries of artillery were placed to dispute any advances from this direction.

A rare steamboat on the river, the *Enterprise,* was sent upstream to tow down some desperately needed barges of ammunition.

Admiral Cochrane was equally busy during these days, planning the destruction of Lieutenant Jones's five gunships, which were guarding the entrance to Lake Borgne with their twenty-three cannon.

From the decks of the eighty-gun *Tonnant*, they looked like bothersome gnats—but they would have to be taken care of, for the deep drafts of the British men-of-war barred them from the lake.

But Cochrane would find a way.

Part VI

You must not sleep until you reach me.
—General Jackson to General John Coffee at
Baton Rouge, December 15, 1814

20

Sea Battle

D URING THE MIDDAY HOURS OF DECEMBER 12, FORTY-FIVE barges and launches were lowered down the steep sides of the British men-of-war to be filled with 1000 seamen and marines. Their objective was the capture or destruction of the American flotilla of gunboats that was barring the way of the British Army over the waters of Lake Borgne.

Captain Nicholas Lockyer, who had called on the Lafittes and participated in the attack on Fort Bowyer, would be in command.

It would be a laborious affair.

Shoving off from their mother ships at three o'clock in the afternoon of a cold December day, the boats, each mounting one gun, would commence the long row toward Lake Borgne and the American ships.

The three divisions of assault boats would stop only when forced to anchor by wind or tide. It would be a long and stressful night followed by a most unpleasant morning.

When Lieutenant Jones realized it was his own flotilla that was the objective of the British, and not a landing attempt, he dispatched the schooner *Seahorse* to Bay St. Louis to salvage the stores there.

But the British were waiting. One division was diverted after *Seahorse*, which held off the British for half an hour under the protection of some shore guns before her commander, Sailing Master Johnson, blew her up along with the stores at Bay St. Louis.

In mid-afternoon, with the British rowing barges closing on his small flotilla, Jones ordered a withdrawal farther into the lake, only to find that three out of the five gunboats were on the ground, including his own flagship. Overboard went everything not needed in the coming fight.

But to no avail.

On came the British crews, toiling at their oars in an attempt to bring the Americans to battle.

But then came the gulf itself to the rescue.

A strong incoming tide freed the stranded vessels so Jones was able to ghost his ships in light winds beyond the British grasp.

But the Americans could not get far in the variable breezes and stayed just beyond the reach of their pursuers.

With dark coming on, Lockyer had to give his oarsmen a break. The collapsing crews slept the night in their boats.

But now the ebbing tide, along with little or no wind, prevented Jones from sailing westward to safety.

With the dawn he had his gunboats anchored in a barrier line that closed off the channel between Malheureux Island and the northern shore, with springs on the cables so the vessels could be swung so their starboard and port broadsides could be delivered in turn against the enemy.

Lockyer, who had roused his crews to their work at 4 A.M., now again was closing on Jones, his exhausted seamen having been at their oars for over forty hours.

It was close to 11 A.M. when the British began to come within long-range fire of the Americans.

But the British did not respond until they closed the range—and the Battle of December 14 erupted in flame.

The Americans were ready with their boarding nets rigged and their largest national battle flags flying, their gunboats soon hidden in the smoke of their own cannon.

But the British were not to be turned back. On they came, with Jones's flagship the main target. Lockyer led the first attack, with his marines cutting the boarding nets to pour out onto the American's decks.

Jones, severely wounded, led his men in savage counterattacks until he fell, unable to continue.

One by one the five small men-of-war were boarded and captured.

Before 1 P.M. it was all over.

British losses were seventeen killed and seventy-seven wounded.

American losses were ten killed, thirty-five wounded, all captured.

Jones had done his duty. He had delayed the mighty British attack.

However, the eastern sea approaches to New Orleans now were open to the enemy.

He would make the most of his chances in a quite unforeseen way.

21

Treachery?

WHEN HE RECEIVED NEWS OF JONES'S SHATTERING DEFEAT on Lake Borgne, Commodore Patterson immediately dispatched a courier to inform Jackson. Old Hickory was with a party of engineers inspecting the approaches to the city from the east by way of the Bayou Chef Menteur, which led to the Gentilly Plain along which the British would find an easy march into New Orleans.

This was the route Old Hickory regarded as the most dangerous.

News of the disaster immediately sent him back to his headquarters.

Emergency actions would be required. Jackson put them into motion.

In this hour of need his thoughts were of his reliable John Coffee and his troops at Baton Rouge. His letter was short and to the point: "You must not sleep until you reach me."

The next day, December 16, he would put New Orleans under martial law.

At the same time Cochrane would move Keane's soldiers thirty miles farther on from the fleet anchorage at Cat Island, to Pea Island off the mouth of the Pearl River, deep into Lake Borgne and much closer to New Orleans.

In addition, acting on secret intelligence furnished from the hostile shore, he sent off Captain Robert Spencer of the navy and Lieutenant John Peddie of the army to conduct a close reconnaissance of the Bayou Bienvenue, which along with its major branch, the Bayou Mazant, would lead into a series of canals extending right up to the Mississippi itself.

When the two officers sailed into the mouth of the Bayou Bienvenue from Pea Island, they made for a collection of shacks on the north bank. There they contacted fishermen expecting them. They were furnished with fishing clothes to hide their uniforms.

From there, their small boat was directed by a guide into the wide bayou. They sailed through a channel bordered by high reeds, which served to screen them from prying eyes.

When they reached the Bayou Mazant, the party turned into its course flowing from the west. After threading a cypress swamp, they emerged into the De La Ronde canal and shortly onto the plantation fields.

They hardly could believe their luck, for they were in sight of the Mississippi levees and about nine miles south of New Orleans.

After completing their reconnaissance, the two officers, their party and the fishermen, with the exception of one sick Spanish fisherman, sailed back to Pea Island to report to a jubilant admiral and general. They had found a way into the American position with not a guard in sight.

While they were reporting, the rowing barges and light draft craft continued the laborious task of transporting the rest of Keane's troops from Cat Island to the Pea Island assembly point.

It had been a most important turning point in the New Orleans campaign.

In the city Jackson was greeted by a unique caller.

Tired of the refusals of his aid to the beleagured town, Jean Lafitte presented himself unannounced at Jackson's door. The two men talked for a long time. When they had finished, Lafitte and his pirates were enrolled in Jackson's defense forces. Jackson needed every man he could get.

Then the next morning, as if by second sight, he ordered Major Gabriel Villeré, who had been given command of a detachment guarding approaches to his father's plantation from the Bayou Bienvenue, to erect obstructions along its course. But the major did not obey his orders. Instead, some three days later, he would send a detachment of twelve men in a boat to "the village of the Spanish fishermen, on the left bank of the Bayou Bienvenue, a mile and a half from its entrance into Lake Borgne, for the purpose of discovering whether the enemy might try to penetrate that way, and to give notice of such attempt."

When they arrived at their post, the sick Spaniard told them all the others were out fishing. The outpost moved into the fishing huts and assigned one sentry to night duty. This continued up until the night of December 22—with no sign of the British. Not a single obstruction was placed on either Bayou Bienvenue or Bayou Mazant.

It would prove a costly blunder.

22

In Stealth and Silence

ON SUNDAY DECEMBER 18, JACKSON REVIEWED HIS troops before a city rife with fear and rumor. The battle on Lake Borgne had not gone well, and the British in immense force were coming ever nearer.

A sick Jackson had to put heart into New Orleans. One sea fight had been lost, but there would be others. And the armies had as yet not been engaged.

A mounted Jackson, splendid in full uniform, impressed the Creoles with his confident demeanor, hiding the dysentery pains that were racking his body.

With drums, bugles and music, New Orleans watched her defenders march past.

Governor Claiborne, with two regiments of Louisiana militia, led the parade of 1500 troops, colorful in their best uniforms. Major Plauché's battalion of New Orleans Volunteers followed to roaring applause, with a battalion of Free Men of Color, composed of Santo Dominican Negroes, closing off the long column.

Maybe it was the troops, maybe it was the music, maybe it was Jackson himself, but something put new spirit into the populace who retired that evening with more confidence in their future.

But there was little rest for Jackson and his lieutenants.

Commodore Patterson readied what naval power he had left with the *Carolina* and *Louisiana,* along with two smaller gunboats, to be retained in front of New Orleans. A third gunboat was sent down to help Fort St. Philip repel any attackers ascending the big river some fifty miles below the city.

Jackson returned to his headquarters to complete the posting of the troops on hand while awaiting the arrival of Coffee and his men, Carroll and his Tennesseans, and Thomas with his Kentuckians.

Meanwhile, General David Morgan would take command of the troops at English Turn fourteen miles to the south, where Fort St. Leon commanded the river.

Dominique Youx and Lafitte's cannoneers would man Fort St. John to the north, guarding the approaches from Lake Pontchartrain.

Other units were spread over the other possible approaches as best their thin strength allowed.

At forbidding Pea Island, with its hundreds of waterfowl and sluggish alligators, General Keane was organizing his striking force into the three brigades that would proceed in stealth and silence to the very doorstep of New Orleans, from where he would launch the thunderstroke that would overwhelm the city.

The first brigade, under Colonel William Thornton, would be the advance unit of the expedition and would include the Eighty-Fifth Light Infantry, the Ninety-Fifth Rifles, parts of the Fourth Light infantry, a rocket detachment and two small three-pound guns. These troops would be sailed and rowed across Lake Borgne to the mouth of Bayou Bienvenue and up it as far as their flat-bottomed barges would go to Bayou Mazant up which they would proceed to the Villeré Canal and the banks of the Mississippi.

While Thornton and his men were crossing the thirty miles of the lake to the bayou, Colonel Francis Brooke would be embarking the second brigade into light transports and gunboats to follow the first brigade across the lake as far as they could proceed. The rowing barges then would return to meet their flotilla, pick up the second brigade and take them up the bayous to join the first brigade. Meanwhile, the third brigade would wait at Pea Island for the return of the gunboats and light transport, for the final ferry of Keane's forces.

Thornton's brigade would be alone below New Orleans until the others could join, but because of the shortage of barges and light draft boats this risk would have to be taken.

Although speed was a prime requisite of the offensive, it would take just so much time to organize the amphibious operation. Hence, it would not be until the morning of December 22 that Thornton's boats would shove off from Pea Island for their long voyage across the lake.

In New Orleans Andrew Jackson, unaware of the surprise the British commanders were preparing for him, used the anxious hours to perfect the defenses as much as he could, still without the services of some of the major portions of his army.

Finally, on the morning of Wednesday December 20, he received the news he had been waiting for when big John Coffee reported he was four miles above New Orleans with eight hundred of his men and the remainder following. They had covered 135 miles in three days.

Old Hickory, who had spent many restless hours on a couch in his headquarters, comforted only by an occasional sip of brandy to ease the pain of his dysentery, sighed in relief. At long last things were coming together.

The day became brighter still with the arrival of Thomas Hinds and his 150 Mississippi Dragoons.

But it brightened even more when late in the afternoon

Carroll's flatboats, filled with 3000 Tennessee troops, were reported off the levees.

The disobedient general also would report that he had with him 1100 muskets taken from a slow-moving contractor on the river, and that his Tennessee blacksmiths had put all arms in good order at their forges and had manufactured "fifty thousand cartridges in the best manner, each containing a musket ball and three buck shot."

With all this good luck, General John Thomas and his 2300 Kentucky riflemen could not be far behind.

Old Hickory was content.

Part VII

Gentlemen, the British are below. We must fight them tonight.
—Andrew Jackson at his headquarters,
December 23, 1814

23

Disaster at Dawn

For the men of Colonel Thornton's First Brigade, the thirty miles they sailed and rowed across Lake Borgne that 22nd of December all had been most miserable ones. Heavy cold rains pelted the open barges throughout the day, sharpened at nightfall by frost, to be relieved only by a brief warming over the charcoal fires kept burning in the sternsheets of each vessel.

Then even this small comfort ended when the fires had to be extinguished later in the evening as the flotilla approached the Louisiana coast. It was close to midnight when the shadowy, rain-drenched armada approached the mouth of Bayou Bienvenue.

With soldiers and sailors cautioned to silence, the crews lay on their oars while the three leading barges were sent ahead to capture the American picket, which by this time had been stationed on the north bank of the wide-mouthed bayou.

After a while the word came back to resume the row up the bayou. The picket had been captured and all was well with the expedition.

The dark serpentine of British barges wound its way up Bienvenue deep into the delta country.

The work at the oars was hard and the progress was slow, but by daylight the leading boats had turned into Bayou Mazant only to finally be stopped by shallow waters.

It was time to put the infantry on its feet.

With Lieutenant Peddie as pathfinder, the advance continued behind a detachment of sappers. General Keane came along, close to the head of the long red-coated column.

In his New Orleans headquarters, Jackson was writing a family letter to Colonel Robert Hays, Rachel's brother-in-law, all unaware of the peril advancing on him. He closed the letter: "since . . . the capture of our gunboats . . . the British have made no movement of importance. . . . All well!"

Things were about to change.

By 10 A.M. the leading regiments, the Eighty-Fifth and Ninety-Fifth, were on the march, leaving the Fourth Regiment disembarking on Mazant.

Shortly thereafter, Jackson had an indication that things were not going all that well in a report from pickets watching on the shores of Lake Borgne. There were "several sail of vessels" in the lake in a position where a landing would threaten the area of the English Turn. The general sent his chief of engineers, Major Latour, to investigate.

Otherwise the morning was calm.

But tension was enveloping the head of the British attack column as it approached the objective of its march.

Before noon the word came down the British line that there were enemy troops ahead.

The head of the column had cleared a cypress swamp and was approaching more open ground. Through some trees could be seen the Villeré plantation house, a wide-spreading one-story structure with twin chimneys.

Some soldiers could be seen loitering around the grounds amid the several outbuildings.

While the rest of the column waited, the Ninety-Fifth Regiment sent forward a detachment of infantry—which in a few moments had captured all the American militiamen on the grounds.

It was a professional operation professionally done. No one was able to escape the net and carry the news to Jackson.

One of those captured was Major Gabriel Villeré, son of the plantation owner and commander of the detachment set to guard the approaches to the Bayous Bienvenue and Mazant. Now he and his men were prisoners in his own house. It was an embarrassment.

Riding south on their mission for Jackson, Chief Engineer Latour and the general's aide, Major Tatum, were crossing the boundary of the De la Ronde and Bienvenue plantations when they met a group of fugitives streaming north. They all told the same astounding story: British troops were at the Villeré plantation just a little farther on. They had captured Gabriel Villeré and all his men.

Latour immediately sent Tatum galloping back to warn Jackson while he went forward to make a close reconnaissance of the enemy's position.

At the Villeré mansion other things were happening. The British guards, now twenty-six hours without sleep, were not as vigilant as they should have been. Gabriel Villeré leapt from the porch of the house and ran across the fields to the De la Ronde plantation. He and Colonel De la Ronde mounted and rode hell-for-leather for New Orleans and Jackson.

However, none of the horsemen would be first to the general, for bad news travels fast.

Jackson was enjoying a noon respite when Augustin Rousseau flung himself from his excited steed in front of army headquarters in Rue Royale and burst in upon him with the incredible news.

The British were eight miles from the city and not a soldier, not a fortification, not a manned obstacle was between them and New Orleans!

How could it be true?

But it was true enough.

Rousseau had ridden through a British skirmish line as it surprised a small militia detachment at the De la Ronde plantation. He was away before the equally surprised Redcoats could halt him.

Jackson was sitting on the edge of his sofa, where he had been resting from the pains of dysentery, listening to Rousseau's shocking report when a sharp rap on the door was followed by the sentry's announcement: "Three gentlemen . . . having important intelligence."

Before him stood three mud-splattered officers: Colonel De la Ronde, Dussau de la Croix and Gabriel Villeré. Major Tatum arrived shortly to join the group.

Their stories told, Jackson's cheeks flushed with his flaming spirit.

He smashed his fist down upon the small table in the bare headquarters room.

"By the Eternal, they shall not sleep on our soil!"

Then regaining control, he calmly invited his visitors to have a glass of wine while he sent for his aides and military secretary.

It was then he announced his decision.

"Gentlemen, the British are below. We must fight them tonight."

24

Counterpunch

WHILE JACKSON'S HEADQUARTERS WAS THE HECTIC SCENE of arriving and departing couriers engaged in carrying orders out to the various commands to bring up the troops, a more tranquil air enwrapped the tired British regiments now deploying across the broad fields of the Lacoste plantation up river from the Villeré mansion where General Keane had set up his headquarters.

Scouting detachments sent north toward the city returned to report that no enemy had been sighted. Outposts immediately were set up to protect the troops from any intrusion from that direction.

A 100-man rear guard was posted down river at the Jumonville plantation. This unit had sighted the enemy when taking up their positions, but the Americans had fled before them.

The exhausted troops prepared to take their first rest and eat their first hot meal since they had left their transports the morning of the previous day.

But while they were stacking their arms for the coming night, Colonel Thornton urged his commander to push the advance on into New Orleans, eight miles above.

He recognized a defenseless city when he saw one.

But Keane would have none of it.

His exhausted and hungry troops were at the end of their tether.

Besides, Brooke should be bringing in his second brigade around midnight with the reserve brigade to file in later.

It was too much of a risk to advance without them.

So with their perimeter guards posted, the red-coated soldiers prepared their bivouac for the night.

Only once was the late afternoon calm disturbed by the bugles calling "to arms" at the appearance of some American mounted scouts, but when they rode away tranquillity returned.

It was not so at Rue Royale.

As soon as he had ordered a night attack, Jackson perfected his plan.

Coffee's division (the Seventh and Forty-Ninth U.S. Infantry), Hinds's Mississippi Dragoons, Pierre Jugeat's Choctaw Indian Battalion, Beale's Rifles, Plauché's New Orleans Battalion, the Free Negro Battalion, and some artillery would conduct the assault. Carroll's Tennessee Division would move up into the city to constitute the reserve.

Patterson would open the show with a bombardment of the British camp from the *Carolina* on their Mississippi River flank at 7:30 P.M. The American ground attack would go in at 8 P.M.

All arrangements were made; all orders understood.

Jackson then went back to the sofa in his headquarters for a nap.

He had done all he could.

None of the combatants could know it, but some hours earlier across the Atlantic in Ghent, Belgium, the British and American delegations had agreed to produce copies of a treaty of peace, to be signed for both nations on Christmas Eve.

25

Night Fight

BY FOUR O'CLOCK JACKSON HAD MOUNTED AND RIDDEN down the levee road in the fading light of a cold December day. The sun beyond the great river was casting long shadows from treetop height. Soon it would be dark.

His latest reports were that the British numbered no more than 2000, had not moved, and apparently were cooking their evening meal before going into camp for the night.

Now Jackson, with little more than 2100 men, was preparing to change their plans.

Off to his left in the growing twilight, Carroll waited in a field of cane stubble with his Tennesseans. Jackson was holding them as his reserve.

To his right, across the dim surface of the great river, he could see shadowy seamen preparing to cast off the moorings that held the schooner *Carolina* to the western bank. Even while he watched, the current began to move her slowly and silently downstream.

It was now past five o'clock with night coming on fast.

With all his troops not yet up, Old Hickory sent Hind's Mississippi Dragoons galloping down the levee road for a last look at the Redcoats. Behind them marched off the Seventh Infantry with orders to engage and halt the British if they were found to be moving north.

Cautiously he decided to move the main body slowly forward, nearer the enemy.

The broad fields of the Bienvenue plantation were crossed. Now in the twilight could be seen the double row of great oak trees leading from the river up to the pretentious chateau named Versailles by the De La Rondes of the next plantation.

Jackson signaled for the columns to halt.

There would be no talking, no noise of any kind.

The Americans now were quite close to the British, a little more than 500 yards away. The British gave no evidence of alarm. Night came down with a mist about the moon.

Keane's campfires were "burning very bright," Jackson wrote, to give "a good view of his situation."

Old Hickory now deployed his fighting line, which extended from the river to beyond the outbuildings of the chateau. The guns along with the marines would stay on the levee, flanked in turn by the Seventh Infantry, the Plauché and Daquin Battalions, and then the Forty-Fourth Infantry on the far left wing.

Coffee would lead his troops out into the blackness of the plain in a wide sweep to the left under guidance of Denis de La Ronde and Pierre Lafitte. Keane's flank and rear would be their objectives.

Returning to the levee about 6:30, Jackson could see the dim outlines of the *Carolina* as she came abreast of his position. He sent his aide, Edward Livingstone, aboard to confirm Patterson's orders to open fire on the British encampment at 7:30 P.M., preceding Jackson's attack one-half hour later.

All of the troops had been inspected for a full supply of ammunition.

The night grew colder over the great river. Men drew their cloaks about them with a shiver of anticipation.

Objects were becoming very hard to see in the darkness. They were made more obscure by a fog rising from the river that had already hidden the *Carolina* and the timid moon.

But the sharp eyes of the British sentries picked out her shrouded bulk as she anchored opposite their encampment. When a series of hails went unanswered, a suspicious soldier fired at the ship.

It was 7:30 on the dot.

Suddenly a brilliant orange glow stained the fog, followed by a thunder of noise as *Carolina* let go with her five six-pounders in her broadside, and her two long twelve-pound swivel cannons on her bow and stern.

In an instant the darkness was filled with screaming shot and shell as Patterson put his men to their work.

What had been a peaceful military encampment offering food and rest to exhausted British troops became a bloody shambles filled with flying death. The *Carolina*'s fire was continuous for half-an-hour of hell for Keane's regiments.

Finally, Colonel Thornton restored some order with the Ninety-Fifth strung out along the river road and the Eighty-Fifth extending their flanks inland. The Fourth was ordered to form a reserve in the vicinity of the Villeré house, Keane's headquarters.

While the cannonade thundered on, Coffee was leading his dismounted troops off to the British flank. Soon the twinkling flashes of gunfire traced his progress as Jackson unleashed his main attack along the levee road promptly at eight o'clock, forcing the British advance guard back behind the De la Ronde canal.

The fighting then became chaos in the dark, every man for himself.

Suddenly a British counterattack drove into the marines protecting the American artillery on the levee. Amid plunging horses and overturned limbers, Jackson rode into the melee.

"Save the guns!"

Marines and soldiers from the Seventh Infantry swarmed to his aid.

The British were thrown back and the artillery was safe.

Out on the black plain, Coffee's troops swept toward the river. They suddenly were attacked by four new companies of Brooke's Second Brigade just arriving on the field. His men were forced back to the north.

At nine o'clock the *Carolina* ceased fire, and gradually the fighting in the dark field lost its fierce intensity.

By midnight it was ominously still.

Jackson pondered the battle.

He knew British reinforcements were coming on the field and that soon he might be facing a far-stronger force.

Besides, his engineers reported there was a very strong position behind an open dry ditch known as the Rodriguez Canal alongside the McCarty plantation some two miles up the river.

Slowly he gave up all thought of a dawn attack and prepared his troops for a gradual withdrawal to the new line. He left only a few cavalry to maintain a screen between himself and the enemy.

This movement got underway in the dark hours of the morning, silent and unseen.

When dawn finally came on December 24, Old Hickory had his men deployed along the new position and the entrenching work had begun.

He counted his casualties at 213, with twenty-four killed and seventy-four missing.

He had little to fear of an immediate pursuit, for Keane had taken a fearful beating. Keane lost 276, of which forty-six were killed and sixty-four missing. His encampment was a mess and his exhausted soldiers still had had no rest.

He and his men faced a bleak Christmas Eve.

26

Peace on Earth?

DECEMBER 24 DAWNED AMID A GRAY BLANKET OF FOG
that obscured the battle positions of both armies.

It was as if an outraged nature had drawn a veil across
the previous night's killing ground.

The British were engaged in clearing up their camp
while the Americans were throwing up heaps of dirt along
the edges of the Rodriguez Canal.

But around eleven o'clock, it would have been fitting if
both combatants had paused to reflect on the course of the
war.

For at six o'clock in Ghent, Belgium, a Treaty of Peace
Between His Britannic Majesty and the United States of
America was being signed by the peace commissioners of
both nations.

Of course, the men on the cutting edge of the struggle,
even now preparing for the greatest battle of the war,

could not know this. They would not know of it for a matter of weeks.

The treaty itself was a poor thing, for it put each country in relatively the same position it had been in when hostilities had opened on June 18, 1812.

But none of this could be known on the fields below New Orleans.

The war would go on.

Part VIII

Pakenham, who distrusted the proceedings of Sir Alexander Cochrane, showed great anxiety on the voyage to arrive at the scene of operations before his troops had been put on shore.
    —Lieutenant Colonel John Fox Burgoyne

27

Belated General

ALL THROUGH THE FOGBOUND FORENOON OF DECEMBER 24, the *Carolina*, now joined by the sixteen-gun converted sloop-of-war *Louisiana* and two of the small gunboats, kept up a constant bombardment on the British encampment. The severity of the bombardment forced Keane to shelter his men behind the levee.

In spite of this harrassment, however, the size of his force continued to grow with the arrival of all of the troops of the Second and Third Brigades by way of the Bayous Bienvenue and Mazant.

Jackson, aware of this growing threat, redoubled the efforts of his men to create a strong defensive position behind the Rodriguez Canal. Still so ill he could only eat a little rice, Old Hickory was in the saddle throughout the day, riding the lines and placing the troops.

He found time to pass orders back to New Orleans for shovels, spades and picks to hurry the works. He also sent for men, horses, wagons and guns. He sent his engineers to survey two fall-back positions upriver to be known as the Line Dupre and the Montreuil Line, much closer to the city.

It now was becoming apparent to his aides that he intended to fight the British below the city, in the city, and above the city if that became necessary. In this he alarmed some of the Creoles, who feared that he would burn New Orleans if the British threatened its capture.

Keane now had on hand all of his force, less his dead and wounded and roughly 200 colored soldiers of the First and Fifth West India regiments who had died from exposure to the unaccustomed cold and freezing rain.

While these activities were engaging the two armies below New Orleans, the general who would be in overall command of the British expedition, Major General Sir Edward Pakenham, was making his belated entrance onto the scene.

On that morning, off to the east near Cat Island, the frigate *Statira* was letting go her anchors near the rest of the heavy ships.

An impatient Pakenham led his aides over the side into Captain Swaine's gig. They then were rowed farther in to the fleet anchorage to go aboard the brig *Anaconda* for a briefing on the latest news from the shore.

There they learned from Sir Thomas Hardy, who had been the immortal Nelson's flag captain aboard HMS *Victory* at Trafalgar, of the British triumph over the American gunboats on Lake Borgne on December 14 and of Keane's landing and advance toward the Mississippi on the previous day. Of course, he had no intelligence of Jackson's attack and the ensuing night battle.

Now more impatient than ever, Pakenham and his staff, although it was ten o'clock at night, boarded a larger boat to set out across Lake Borgne for the cold, long voyage to the mouth of Bayou Bienvenue. After a frigid night they sighted Cochrane's red ensign flying from the fishermen's wretched huts at the entrance to the wide-mouthed bayou.

Ashore, Cochrane and his chief of staff, Admiral Codrington, who had been one of Nelson's captains at Trafalgar, welcomed the tired and salt-stained travelers to breakfast.

While they were eating, Cochrane briefed them on the landing, the advance march and the seizure of the Villeré plantation by Keane's troops. He also furnished them the information he had on the night battle of December 23.

Now in an agony of apprehension about the condition of his army, Pakenham, along with Major General Gibbs; his engineer, Lieutenant Colonel Burgoyne; his artillerist, Colonel Dickson; and his aide, Captain Alexander Campbell Wylly; boarded two waiting gigs to sail and row up the Bayou Bienvenue to the troops.

Colonel Dickson wrote of the trip:

> The creek has a great many turns and reaches in it, and the whole way up is covered on each side by high reeds, it is of a good breadth for four or five miles, and then narrows so much, and is so shallow, that the boats cannot row for want of room, and are pushed through the mud by means of the oars shoving against the bank. About a mile above the Huts (Cochrane's headquarters) there are two broad creeks, one running away into the Marsh to the right (Upper Bienvenue), and the other to the left (Mazant), and all the way up there are on both sides a number of little Channels or inlets, full of water, which would render moving along the bank impossible, even where it is hard enough. From the landing place to (Keane's) Head Quarters is about 2½ Miles, the road being nothing more than a very bad and boggy path along the bank of a little canal . . . which extends from the Creek nearly to the Mississippi, and is navigable for Canoes to within 1000 yards of the river, this is named the Bayou Villaré [sic], being for the use of that plantation. The Road for the distance of ¾ of a mile from the landing place is through Reeds and the ground Consequently very boggy, it then enters a thick wood about 1¼ miles across . . . the

wood is generally of Cypress trees growing closely together, and full of thick Brush and Palmettos, the bottom being swampy with deep holes interspersed, full of water, it is therefore in every respect impracticable. From the edge of the wood to Villaré's plantation the distance is about half a Mile of tolerably good and broad road, and from the Plantation to the bank of the river is about 300 yards. A party is employed in improving this road.

It was over this route that the navy already had boated and dragged twelve cannons and three brass howitzers of the marine artillery.

Ending their boat trip about eleven o'clock, Pakenham and his party arrived at Keane's headquarters sometime after one o'clock on Christmas day.

It would not be a happy holiday.

28

Dead End?

WHEN PAKENHAM GOT OUT INTO THE BATTLEFIELD OF the December 23 night battle to inspect his troops, he found the American schooner *Carolina* and two smaller gunboats lobbing shells into the British position. The larger *Louisiana* upstream posed an even greater threat to Keane's left flank should she come down the river with her more powerful armament.

The general found his men's spirits high in spite of the losses suffered in the confused battle, the continued harrassment of the American naval guns from the river and the prowling patrols of Jackson's sharpshooters during the night hours that made sleep all but impossible and kept nerves on edge.

But the army's position, with one flank on the river open to American attack and the other on a cypress swamp that inhibited any kind of maneuver other than a straight-ahead attack on what he assumed were constantly strengthening fortified lines, was not a heartening one.

Then there was the line of supply back to the fleet: seventy miles across the wide and sometimes turbulent waters of Lake Borgne, to be followed by the miserable, muddy and laborious passage up Bayou Bienvenue and Bayou Mazant.

Cochrane and Keane had found a hidden way deep into the enemy's position. But once there, what was the army to do?

That was Pakenham's problem.

At the same time the general was making his first survey of the field, the artillerist, Colonel Dickson, was being shown over the ground by the navy's senior officer with the advance, Rear Admiral Pulteney Malcolm. Dickson immediately learned that the artillery was woefully short of ammunition.

He also saw there was a way to get at Patterson's gadfly schooner *Carolina,* which was raising so much hell with the troops. When he met back at the Villeré House with Pakenham to agree that nothing much could be done until this naval gunfire could be eliminated, he told the general that he could do it.

How?

Cut embrasures in the levee opposite the *Carolina,* anchored 800 yards away. Then when the two nine-pound and four six-pound guns and the two five-and-one-half inch howitzers were mounted in them, open with surprise fire. With a little luck the artillery expert hoped to bag the ship.

Pakenham told him to go ahead.

Before dawn of December 26, Dickson was ready with his guns hidden in the levee under a blanket of cane trash, ready to fire on order.

The ground troops were organized into a right flank brigade under the command of Major General Sam Gibbs that included the Fourth, Forty-Fourth, Twenty-First and the First West India Regiment; and a left flank brigade under Major General John Keane to include the Eighty-Fifth, Ninety-Third, Ninety-Fifth and the Fifth West India Regiment.

Pakenham and Dickson went forward to inspect the outposts held by the light infantry under Colonel Thornton, where a rampart had been built at the Lacoste plantation house a half mile in advance of the army headquarters at the Villeré mansion.

The two officers then went 300 yards farther on to join a squad of pickets sheltering in two outbuildings to see if they could get a view of Jackson's fortified line. While they could see much of the plain, the actual Rodriguez Canal line was hidden from their view by a bend in the river.

While they were observing through their glasses, American horsemen appeared and set fire to standing sugar cane stalks and cane trash, evidently to clear fields of fire for the defenders.

Dickson, in commenting on the fiery blaze, said, ". . . this will be to our advantage as it clears the ground for our advancing."

He also detailed results of a cut in the levee made by the Americans the night before for the purpose of flooding the British position. But in this they had failed, for instead of making the cut above the British lines to flood out their routes of advance, it had been made below the army headquarters with little or no damage.

Dickson reported:

> . . . a party of the Enemy either came across the water, or up by land from Detour des Anglois, and made a cut in the Levee, not more than 151 or 200 Yards distance from our piquet on the great road below Head Quarters. By this Cut which was very deep, the Water was admitted from the river into the plain and it was rushing in very strongly, when discovered by Genl. Keane this morning, and a strong working party being immediately sent, the Gap was filled up. This was so great a Neglect on the part of the piquet,

which had been ordered to Patrole along the Levee every hour during the night, that the officer Commanding A Captain MacLean of the 21st regt. has been put in arrest by order of Sir Edward Pakenham.

When the *Carolina* fired on a building marked and used by the British as a hospital, the enraged general ordered Dickson to turn his levee guns loose on her. The artillerist disagreed, recommending ". . . to defer it to the morning early, when we shall take the Enemy by Surprise."

Upon the arrival of a small addition of artillery ammunition, Dickson wrote, ". . . our prospect of supply is very disheartening. We must be Economical in our expenditure upon the Schooner, as otherwise I fear we shall have no Gun Ammunition when the Army advances."

To the north Jackson was having his own problems.

The Rodriguez Canal actually was an old abandoned millrace, grown over with grass and weeds. It stretched from the levee inland for almost a thousand yards to a stubby growth of moss-hung cypress trees edging into slimy swampland. Throughout its length, the ditch, for that was all it was, was about twelve feet wide with sides varying from four to eight feet deep.

Behind this obstacle Jackson put his troops and 900 Negro slaves to work raising an embankment to protect its defenders. Because the ground was so soggy, stakes and fence rails were driven into the earth. Soil excavated and brought forward from the rear was piled against them.

Beginning this work immediately after the December 23 night battle, Old Hickory could see the trace of a rampart beginning to form at sundown on Christmas Eve. The entrenchment continued on through the night and the days and nights following, with the troops sleeping on their arms while their fellow soldiers toiled on.

Jackson was everywhere riding the line. For three critical nights he did not go to bed; he took short naps where and when he could.

On the left, Coffee's men had begun to fell trees to extend a log rampart 600 yards farther into the swamp.

But the fortifications did not impress some of the Creoles, who reported to their New Orleans friends that it was nothing but a mud line rampart.

Some of the legislators now sitting in the city were rumored to be discussing disaffection and the possible surrender of the city to the British.

Luckily for them, Old Hickory had heard none of these reports as yet.

One of the first things Pakenham and Dickson had done after arriving at the battlefield was to order more heavy guns to be brought forward from the fleet along with furnaces to heat shot to be used on the *Carolina.* It was at two o'clock on the nasty, rainy, foggy morning of December 27 that Dickson's gunners were busy before their flaming furnaces heating the shot that would be used against the schooner when the new day dawned.

The artillerist was an expert in the use of hot shot, having set fire to the French magazine at Salamanca in the Peninsular War. For this he won credit from Wellington for one of the key actions forcing the surrender of that fortress.

Just before eight o'clock in the fog and the rain, Dickson gave the gunners the command to open fire through the levee embrasures with the nine-pounders throwing red-hot shot at the *Carolina,* while the six-pounders and the heavy howitzers joined in.

Dickson knew his business, for the guns were on their target almost immediately. The *Carolina,* beset with the flaming shot, got off a few shots in return before the crew was forced to abandon ship and head for the river bank.

Jackson witnessed the cannonade from the galleries of the Macarty plantation mansion, where he had established his headquarters just behind the Rodriguez Canal ramparts. Through his glass he could see that the *Carolina* was doomed, but almost just as imperiled was the larger *Louisiana* just upriver from her consort.

Jackson ordered her towed upstream and saved at any cost.

At about 10:30 the *Carolina*, burning ever more fiercely, blew up in a thunderous explosion, throwing her burning timbers high in the air and raining fiery debris all about the river and its banks.

Dickson now turned his gunners' efforts to the *Louisiana* at about the guns' extreme range of more than a mile upriver. But the American sailors in her boats bent mightily to their oars, especially after one red-hot shot smashed down her quarterdeck.

Then she slowly was towed out of danger, setting off a loud cheering from Jackson's soldiers watching the show.

In the bombardment Dickson had used roughly a third of his available ammunition, but true to his word, he had removed *Carolina*'s waterborne threat to Pakenham's flank.

As the sun went down, Old Hickory's sixth sense warned him that another dangerous thrust was coming. Could he parry it?

29

Opening Guns

PAKENHAM'S FIRST ATTEMPT ON THE RODRIGUEZ CANAL
line began at first light on December 28 with a two-
pronged infantry advance. One column, under Keane,
moved along the levee road against the American right
flank. A second column thrust forward against the American left under General Gibbs.

The day was clear and cold, so Jackson, watching the
development of the action from the galleries of the Macarty mansion, had a fine view of the British columns as
they advanced to their work.

Master Commandant Daniel Patterson also had a fine
view from the deck of the *Louisiana*, which had been
brought down river to bring flanking fire on any British
advance on the American line. He waited tensely until
Keane's Redcoats were within about 500 yards of the mud

ramparts. Ignoring the shell splashes in the Mississippi, where the British artillery was searching for his ship, Patterson ordered his gunners to open fire.

The whole of *Louisiana*'s starboard battery blasted into action, joined by five cannon firing from the mud line.

The effect was instantaneous.

A British lieutenant wrote:

> Scarce a ball passed over or fell short of its mark, but all striking full into the midst of our ranks, occasioned terrible havoc, The shrieks of the wounded, therefore, the crash of firelocks, and the fall of such as were killed, caused at first some little confusion; and what added to the panic was, that from the houses beside which we stood bright flames suddenly burst out. . . . The scene was altogether very sublime. A tremendous cannonade moved down our ranks, and deafened us with its roar; whilst two large chateaux and their outbuildings almost scorched us with the flames, and blinded us with the smoke which they emitted.

Keane ordered the brigade to deploy and take cover while Dickson ordered forward his own artillery to bring fire on the *Louisiana* and the American guns firing from the rampart.

Pakenham galloped into the action and ordered Keane and Dickson to keep up the pressure on the American line while he scouted the American defenses on their left.

Then, riding to the forward edge of Gibbs's advance skirmish line, he and Dickson dismounted to go forward on foot to canvass the ground. Although it seemed that Gibbs's column might have a chance to turn the American flank, Pakenham told Gibbs to erect protection for his forward batteries while Dickson brought up more artillery in support.

On the other side of the line, Jackson, seeing the danger to his left, was riding off to bring more aid to Coffee and Carroll. Suddenly he was halted by one of his volunteer aides, an Abner Duncan of New Orleans, who shouted out that Governor Claiborne had sent him to inform Jackson that the legislature was about to vote surrender to the enemy.

When Jackson was told that the source of the information was Colonel Declouet, Jackson thundered in rage that he be put under arrest.

Even though Gibbs's column was within a half mile of Jackson's left flank and beginning to deploy for attack, Duncan insisted in his errand:

"The governor expects orders what to do!"

An angry Jackson, turning in his saddle, shouted over his shoulder:

"I don't believe the intelligence, but tell the governor to make an inquiry . . . and if they persist to blow them up!"

With that he put his horse into a gallop toward where Carroll and Coffee were facing the full force of Gibbs's long red-coated column.

What had happened was that Duncan had completely misunderstood what Declouet, a Creole colonel of one of the Louisiana regiments, had told him when he reported suspected treasonable rumors of surrender current in the legislature in New Orleans. They were rumors—nothing more—but Duncan had taken them to the stage of action.

During Jackson's ride to the left, Dickson's artillery and Congreve rocket batteries were plastering the American position with extremely heavy fire, which was terrifying to those many hundreds of new recruits who had never been in battle. Officers rode the rampart on rearing mounts attempting to calm the troops.

But while Keane's attack column was trying to sort itself out from the disarray into which it had been plunged by the *Louisiana*'s telling flank fire from the river, Gibbs's skirmish lines advanced with overpowering force against the Tennesseans on the left of the long rampart. Then just when the British infantry expected to be ordered to assault with bayonets, they were halted.

After taking whatever cover they could find, they eventually were ordered to withdraw amid discontented muttering from the troops. They couldn't understand it.

Pakenham finally drew new lines along the Chalmette plantation, halfway between Villeré's and the Rodriguez Canal.

During this unexpected suspension of the British attack on his left, Jackson rode back to his headquarters in the Macarty mansion to find Senator Bernard Marigny, his anger cooled somewhat by his long wait for Jackson, demanding an explanation for the forcible closure of the Louisiana legislature.

Jackson was astounded. He had sent no such orders to Governor Claiborne.

It was Duncan again. When he returned to New Orleans, he had taken it upon himself to tell Claiborne that Jackson wished the legislature suspended.

Satisfied by Jackson's explanations, the senator finally asked the all-important question.

What were the general's plans for the city of New Orleans if he and his army were forced to retreat?

Jackson paused for some time before he answered.

If I thought the hair on my head knew my thoughts on that subject I would cut if off and burn it. . . . Return to your Honorable body and say to them from me, that if I was so unfortunate to be beaten from they [sic] lines . . . and compelled to retreat through New Orleans, they could have a warm session.

With that the emissary from the legislature had to be content.

But Marigny had seen the British attacks repelled or suspended, so he felt much cheered by the prospects during his ride back to the city.

The same could not be said for General Keane, who commanded the British column of the left. When Pakenham and Dickson ordered two additional six-pounders to assist his advance, the new guns were taken under fire by American artillery either on the ramparts or the *Louisiana* and damaged so they could not be used.

Keane's infantry were under the American fire for seven hours before the thunder of battle died away.

During the day Jackson had 3,282 men behind the mud ramparts while the British counted about 5,500 in their attack.

Pakenham would call the operation a "Reconnaissance in Force."

But he had lost the second battle for New Orleans.

30

Massed Artillery

PAKENHAM NOW FACED A BITTER PROBLEM. KEANE'S stealthy advance to the Mississippi had been wrecked by the counter-surprise Jackson unexpectedly had hurled at him in the night battle of December 23.

Now his own double-headed thrust at the American lines on December 28 had been parried skillfully by effective use of infantry and artillery fighting from prepared positions.

As yet his army had been unable to effect a lodgment or penetration of any kind in the enemy position.

What to do?

There were two answers. Both had to do with increased force, either in infantry or artillery.

Pakenham would get more infantry with the arrival of Lambert's brigade, which was expected momentarily.

But the artillery could only come from the fleet, and the fleet was nearly seventy miles away.

Never mind, he would have that artillery.

Then the British Army and Navy staged a military miracle.

By nightfall of December 28, two of the heavy and cumbersome eighteen-pound naval cannon had made the dangerous and difficult voyage and traverse to the banks of the Mississippi. More were to follow.

The effort involved the lowering of the heavy cannon down the steep sides of the men-of-war into open barges, which then would be rowed across the unpredictable waters of Lake Borgne to the Bayou Bienvenue to Bayou Mazant. From there they would be transported along the difficult and muddy path leading up to the Villeré plantation. Once there, they had to be hauled to their places on the field under concealment until the moment came to emplace them in darkness 800 yards from the enemy line. It was a monumental task calling for sheer strength and muscle power. But it was done.

The results of this tremendous effort were impressive.

By nightfall of December 28 two eighteen-pound cannon had been dragged up to the left flank of the army close to the levee. They would be placed in battery with facilities to fire up hot shot for them by the following night.

Over the next two days and nights, the navy would transport eight more eighteen-pounders and four twenty-four-pound monster guns for use in Pakenham's artillery assault.

Colonel Dickson and his artillery teams laid out and sighted the battery positions that would be occupied during the night hours prior to the delivery of the grand bombardment. All field transport was accomplished by use of plantation wagons and carts except for the twenty-four-pounder carronades, which were manhandled all the way from the boats on their own massive carriages.

This operation entailed the use of "near two kegs of

grease" to ease the friction generated by their heavy weight on rocks and gravel on the road, and so prevent the guns from setting fire to themselves.

Dickson set up a manufactory for cartridges behind the lines, combing all the abandoned plantation houses for "hangings, bed curtains, sheeting etc., that would answer, and a detachment of tailors, part from the Artillery, and part from the line, were set to work to make Cartridge bags."

Because water in the ground prevented the digging of emplacements for the guns, sugar casks were filled with earth and dirt thrown over them to provide this protection.

At nightfall on New Year's Eve, Dickson's artillerymen and Burgoyne's engineers stood ready to begin this work.

Two eighteen-pounders, to rain shot and shell on Jackson's right flank, were emplaced on the levee road. Then running off to the British right and the cypress woods, sailors, marines and infantry labored to put into position in sequence three five-and-one-half-inch mortars with the rocket battery to their fore; then a seven-gun battery of two nine-pounders, three six-pounders, and two five-and-one-half-inch howitzers; then six eighteen-pounders and four twenty-four-pound carronades stretched along a road from the center.

It was a most powerful array of some thirty guns and rockets ready to batter holes in the mudline rampart. But none of them had a full day's supply of ammunition, so they must achieve their purpose of cutting out a path for the infantry early on.

Installation of the guns would begin at darkness on New Year's Eve and was to be completed before dawn on New Year's Day.

Dickson directed all the work himself and reported that the gun platforms were "ill laid, uneven, and unsteady, but in finding these faults, it is but justice to add, that under existing circumstances no more could possibly have been done in the time."

If the British were busy, the Americans were equally so during the three days and nights following the repulse of Pakenham's first thrust at their line. At the center of the whirlwind of activity was Jackson, defying the pains of dysentery that were wracking his spare frame.

With guns and entrenching tools commandeered from the city of New Orleans, the mudline rampart was further strengthened and more troops had weapons in their hands.

But it was to his artillery that Jackson devoted most of his attention.

Commodore Patterson emplaced two twenty-four-pounders across the river from the city and two twelve-pounders behind the levee opposite Jackson's main line.

On the mudline ramparts Jackson increased his artillery from five to twelve, counting one thirty-two pounder, three twenty-four pounders, one long brass eighteen-pounder, three twelve-pounders, three six-pounders, and a six-inch heavy howitzer. Using 150 bales of cotton, his engineers and artillerymen built firm and level platforms for the ordnance, paying particular attention to the left flank that had been so threatened by General Sam Gibbs's advance against Coffee and Carroll on December 28.

Credit for the key role in strengthening the American lines was given to Jackson by his chief engineer, Latour, who wrote:

> Although . . . ready to sink under the weight of sickness and fatigue, his mind never lost for a moment that energy which caused insurmountable obstacles" [to melt before him. This] "energy . . . spread . . . to the whole army . . . composed of heterogeneous elements . . . speaking different languages, and brought up in different habits . . . There was nothing . . . it did not feel capable of doing if he ordered it to be done.

But in all this Jackson never lost sight of his need to control the battlefield itself.

By day his artillery dropped random fire along the British lines. By night his frontiersmen, working in "hunting parties," stalked sentries and made life miserable for the Redcoats wherever they could.

Jackson began to feel confident of his ability to throw back the invader—maybe too confident—for he ordered a formal review to be held behind the lines on New Year's Day. To this event invitations were sent out to the citizens of New Orleans.

New Year's Eve blanketed both armies in fog and deep darkness.

If one listened carefully, he might hear the pound of sledges of the British engineers and artillerymen installing their batteries.

But on this night no one on the American side noted these ominous sounds.

31

New Year's Cannonade

NEW YEAR'S DAY 1815 CAME TO NEW ORLEANS AND THE troops contending for her possession shrouded in rain and fog. Jackson had been out on his long line early in the cold damp of the river mist, but with nothing unusual happening before his ramparts he retreated to his couch in the Macarty house. He rested briefly before his grand review behind the lines, which would display to his troops their own strength and bolster the confidence of the Creole society of New Orleans in their defenders.

Soldiers were busy with their equipment and their uniforms, a band was playing, and it appeared that the new year would be welcomed in grand style. Some of the guests from the city, including some handsomely gowned ladies, began to arrive with their escorts.

There was a festive air for the first time on the long, grim mud-packed line.

For a brief moment, as he lay on the couch, Jackson felt confident and content.

Then suddenly the world blew apart.

The Macarty house rocked on its foundations.

Windows shattered glass in all directions.

With the British artillery thundering shot and shell over his entire line, Jackson made his way to the door amid falling plaster and glass. Soldiers were running to the ramparts. The review guests were seeking shelter where they could find it.

The commanding general could see that the fog was lifting, but he also could see that there was not going to be a parade.

Pakenham had touched off his latest attempt on the Rodriguez Canal line, which stood between him and New Orleans.

Under a blaze of rocket fire, Jackson made his way to the guns on the levee flank of the rampart. There he spoke to Captain Humphrey of the regulars, commander of the battery who "dressed in his usual plain attire and smoking that eternal cigar was cooly levelling his guns." Because of the low silhouette presented by the sugar barrels and the earth thrown over them in protection of the British batteries, it was some time before the casual captain was satisfied with the aim of his twelve-pounders.

Finally turning to his gunners, he gave his assent.

"Let her off."

The American line now was responding to the tremendous British barrage.

At Battery Three Lafitte's brother, Dominique Youx, who had been hit in his arm by a shell fragment while examining the enemy position through his glass, turned to Jackson as the general came up.

"I'll make them pay for that!" he promised his chief.

The British fire was finding targets, silencing a thirty-two and a twelve-pounder.

Rockets exploded a caisson filled with ammunition, which got a cheer from the British infantry waiting in columns on their two flanks to exploit the first sign of weakness in the mud-line rampart.

Smoke and noise enveloped the battlefield, some of the smoke billowing out from the embrasures of the American artillery where protecting cotton bales around the guns had been set on fire.

Try as they would, however, the British cannon could not silence the American guns.

Only one ground thrust was aimed at Jackson's line during the entire bombardment, which roared on for more than three hours. Then Lieutenant Colonel Rennie of the Twenty-First Regiment led a strong detachment into the swamp on the left, where after driving in the American pickets, he waited for Pakenham's signal for a general assault. It never came and his men were withdrawn from their advanced position when the guns finally fell silent—because the British artillery ran out of ammunition.

Colonel Dickson noted in his after-action report in his journal that his fire "only ceased for want of Ammunition, for we had not one piece of heavy Ordnance disabled or even struck."

But he added, ". . . even if there had been Sufficient Ammunition, the nature of our Batteries were such the men could not have gone on for many hours longer." The gun platforms built during the night hours were proving "uneven and loose," and the eighteen-pound naval guns mounted on their heavy wooden carriages designed for a ship's deck "were found very Awkward and unmanageable."

As a result he was forced to report "during the Cannonade, or at least until the latter part of it, our fire did not attain the precision it ought, neither could it be kept up with the rapidity necessary to Silence the Enemies Guns."

Behind the mudline rampart in his ruined headquarters in the Macarty house, Jackson was issuing an order to his army:

"The Major General tenders to the troops he has the honor to command his good wishes for a happy new year, and especially to those officers & men at the pieces of Artillery. . . . Watch Word Fight on—The Contractor will issue half a gill of whiskey around."

But the battle did not end when Pakenham cancelled all plans for an infantry assault, for the British had many of their cannon exposed in their forward positions from which they must be withdrawn.

This was going to be made more difficult by heavy rains sweeping the sodden field during the afternoon.

Early on New Year's night the lighter guns were pulled back to safety without too much trouble. But the heavy ordnance was going to prove much more difficult.

Two eighteen-pounders were withdrawn after a struggle, leaving only the central battery of ten heavy guns, which were rapidly being mired in the drenching rains and mud.

Finally, the soldiers detailed to the thankless task, dispirited by the aborted battle, wet to the skin and knee deep in mud, began to steal away into the night.

Dickson trudged to the Lacoste house, where Pakenham was sleeping, to ask for aid. Major Harry Smith, his adjutant general, roused him. Along with the artillerist, they made their way back through the rain and night to the beleagured guns, where through the exhortations of their commanding general, the soldiers finally returned to the task of hauling out the muddy monsters.

This was accomplished before the wet and miserable dawn.

The breakdown in discipline reflected the dispirited state of the army.

Major Smith noted: "Poor Sir Edward was much mortified at being obliged to retire the army from a second demonstration and disposition to attack, but there was nothing for it."

Lieutenant George Robert Gleig wrote:

For two whole nights and days not a man had closed an eye, except such as were cool enough to sleep amidst showers of cannon-ball; and during the day scarcely a moment had been allowed in which we were able so much as to break our fast. We retired, therefore, not only baffled and disappointed, but in some degree disheartened and discontented. All our plans had as yet proved abortive; even this, upon which so much reliance had been placed, was found to be of no avail; and it must be confessed that something like murmuring began to be heard through the camp.

Admiral Codrington, Cochrane's naval chief of staff, decried the failure of the artillery to win their battle as "not to be expected . . . and a blot on the artillery escutcheon."

Pakenham now was putting all his faith on the arrival of General John Lambert's brigade to give him the added power necessary to break Jackson and his stubborn American defenders.

Both sides suffered comparatively light losses in the long artillery battle. The Americans lost eleven killed and twenty-three wounded. British losses were thirty-two killed, forty-two wounded and two missing.

In reporting to Secretary of War James Monroe on January 3, 1815, Old Hickory wrote:

> The enemy occupy their former position and are engaged in strengthening it; Our time is spent in the same employment and in exchanging long shot with them. . . . I do not know what may be their further design—Whether to redouble their efforts, or apply them elsewhere. . . . I am preparing for either event.

Jackson himself was looking for reinforcements in the long-awaited arrival of General Thomas and his Kentucky division. For him they could not come too soon.

In any event, Sir Edward Pakenham had lost the third battle for New Orleans.

Part IX

That fatal ever fatal rocket.
      —British officer before American line at
            New Orleans, January 8, 1815

32

Men Without Arms

THERE WOULD BE ANOTHER BLOW. JACKSON FELT IT IN HIS bones.

But where?

To insure against another surprise, he strengthened his two reserve lines to the rear and became more concerned about a flanking attempt from the west bank of the river where he had stationed Brigadier General David B. Morgan with 550 of the Louisiana militia. These troops were positioned behind a shallow ditch with none of the natural strength of the Rodriguez Canal line.

From captured prisoners and deserters he had learned that Pakenham expected heavy reinforcements with the arrival of Major General Lambert's brigade from Jamaica. But where would they be used against Jackson's already overextended lines?

Where were his own long-expected reinforcements, even now overdue on their flatboat voyage down the Mississippi?

He got the answer to this question on January 4 when General Thomas led the advance contingent of his division across the New Orleans levees. But when his aide, Livingstone, reported them poorly clothed and most of them without arms, Old Hickory was astounded.

"I don't believe it," he said. "I have never seen a Kentuckian without a gun and a pack of cards and a bottle of whiskey in my life!"

But it was true enough. Thomas could count only 700 rifles or muskets for 2,368 men.

Old Hickory already had complained to Secretary Monroe:

> The Arms I have been so long expecting have not yet Arrived. All we hear of them is that . . . the man entrusted with their transportation has halted on the way for the purpose of private speculations. . . . This negligence . . . threatens the defeat of our armies.

Meanwhile, on January 2, Lambert's brigade had arrived on transports at the fleet's main anchorage off Cat Island.

Lambert reported at Pakenham's headquarters the next day with his Seventh and Forty-Third Regiments following to take their places on the New Orleans line on January 4—the same day Thomas's Kentucky troops were arriving up river at New Orleans.

To protect their Kentucky defenders from the cold and rain, the Louisiana legislature voted $16,000 for blankets, which then were cut and shaped into clothing by the ladies of New Orleans.

Jackson's chief engineer noted:

> Within one week twelve hundred blanket cloaks, two hundred and seventy-five waistcoats, eleven hundred and twenty-seven pairs of pantaloons, eight hundred shirts, four hundred and ten pairs of shoes, and a great number of

mattresses, were made up, or purchased ready made, and distributed among our brethren in arms, who stood in the greatest need of them.

Old Hickory, still jumpy over surprise attacks on his rear and flanks, sent Dragoon Reuben Kemper and a party of eleven men northeast to scout the Piernas Canal leading to the Mississippi from the northern reaches of the Bayou Bienvenue. Taking two canoes, he went down the canal to the bayou without sighting any enemy.

Emboldened by his progress, he went down the bayou to its junction with the Bayou Mazant. There he observed that the British had a fortified camp. Leaving his canoes and most of his men, he then went forward on foot and in the reeds, he looked out upon a line of British boats closing off the upper Mazant.

Discovered on his return to the canoe by Captain James Laurence of the British ship *Alceste,* he escaped with all but one of his men to report to Jackson that for the moment his rear in that direction was not threatened.

To a haggard Old Hickory, the intentions of his opponent still were obscured.

33

Now or Never

WHILE AWAITING THE ARRIVAL OF MAJOR GENERAL JOHN Lambert and his brigade of the Seventh and the Forty-Third Regiments, Pakenham had been busy perfecting a new plan to use his additional force to overrun Jackson's line and capture the city of New Orleans. It would be quite different from those of the two previous attacks.

What the thousands of troops on the Rodriguez Canal Line and the men and women of the beleagured city could not know was that far out in the Atlantic, His Britannic Majesty's frigate *Brazen* was battling stormy seas while making her way to America with the most important news of the War of 1812: the signing of the treaty of peace at Ghent. She would not arrive to send her boats off to the flagship *Tonnant*, lying off Mobile Bay, until February 13, 1815.

When Lambert reported to him at the Villeré mansion on January 3, Pakenham lost no time in acquainting him with the new attack plan, which would involve him in a leading role.

Work to implement the plan began almost immediately following the cannonade of New Year's Day. This was to cut a wider and deeper Villeré Canal all the way from the landing place at the Bayou Mazant to the Mississippi River, so that boats loaded with infantry could be brought up the Bayou Bienvenue to the Bayou Mazant and from there to the canal and along the canal to the levee. There a cut would be made through which they could pass out upon the river for an attack against Morgan's troops and their enfilading flank fire batteries on the west bank of the river.

Once this position had been captured, the guns would be turned on Jackson's troops. With a little luck, they would sweep clean much of the defenses of the mud line rampart.

At the same time a powerful ground attack would break Jackson's defenses.

It was an ingenious plan that featured surprise combined with heavy firepower. It was dependent on swift execution under cover of darkness and close coordination between the two attacks on each side of the river.

The first requirement would be to open the waterway for Colonel Thornton's boats loaded with 1100 men so they could be rowed across the black waters of the Mississippi to launch their surprise attack on General Morgan's unsuspecting and ill-defended position behind the western levee.

The canal widening and deepening scheme had been devised by Admiral Cochrane, with the army digging in shifts.

The assault on Jackson's main line would be delivered by Gibbs's brigade on the enemy left. Keane's brigade would attack along the levee against the American right. Lambert's brigade would follow in the center, ready to exploit any opportunity offered.

Thornton's across-the-river expedition would be dubbed the "fourth brigade." It would include a rocket detachment that would be used against New Orleans if things went well on the west bank with the capture of Morgan's guns and the destruction of his defense line.

Gibbs' column would include Fourth, Twenty-First and Forty-Fourth Regiments, with the Forty-Fourth carrying fascines of brush to throw in the ditch and ladders to surmount the ramparts. Its own light infantry would guard the right flank against any attack from the cypress woods.

Keane's river column would count the Forty-Third and Ninety-Third Regiments, with Colonel Rennie's light companies designated to capture a redoubt that against Jackson's better judgments had been built alongside the levee forward of the main line. Once in the redoubt, his troops would spike the American guns designed to bring flanking fire on the British attack.

Lambert's own brigade in the center would be a powerful force, including the Seventh, Forty-Third, part of the West India Regiment, and the Fourteenth Light Dragoons dismounted.

All in all it was a most imposing array of power. If things went well, it should be enough to do the job. It would be supported by Dickson's repaired and resupplied artillery.

Some of the round shot had been carried from the fleet in the knapsacks of Lambert's infantrymen. This provided a valuable contribution to the artillery.

But there had been one unfortunate accident when one of the *Statira*'s boats, loaded with seventeen fusiliers, capsized on Lake Borgne. The soldiers dropped to the bottom because of the weight of the shot they carried.

To assist Thornton's river crossing, Dickson sighted batteries of six eighteen-pounders and two twenty-four-pound carronades to support his attack on Morgan and also discourage any waterborne artillery attack by Jackson's forces.

The rest of the considerable artillery was positioned to assist the infantry brigades in their assaults on the American main line.

Although the attack originally had been planned to go forward on January 7, the canal still was not deep enough or wide enough to accommodate Thornton's boats.

Therefore, it was postponed to January 8, 1815.

Jackson began to get some indications of Pakenham's plans on January 6 when Navy Sailing Master Johnson captured and burned a small British transport schooner on Lake Borgne. He learned from the ten prisoners he took that the British were extending the Villeré Canal to the Mississippi River.

When he heard this report, Jackson ordered 400 of the Kentucky troops across the river to support Morgan on the night of January 7. Half of these troops were unarmed.

During the day Jackson had observed through his telescope from the upper gallery of the Macarty mansion that the British troops were busy on what looked to be fascines and "working on pieces of wood, which we concluded must be ladders."

After nightfall, the sound of the British installation of their batteries could be heard.

The commanding general went to bed convinced that the morrow would be the day.

34

Night and Fog

AFTER ORDERING HALF HIS FORCE TO MAN THE RAMPARTS while the other half slept, Jackson sought sleep himself on the floor of a room in the Macarty house, surrounded by his aides. They lay down fully dressed, only sword belts unbuckled and pistols ready to hand.

But the troubled night barely had begun its black march toward dawn when Jackson stirred at the sound of someone whispering to the sentry in the hall.

"Who's there?" he asked.

The sentry admitted a courier from Commandant Patterson with a message reporting heavy enemy units massing along the banks of the levee, ready to cross the Mississippi to the western bank.

Fearing an attack on General Morgan's position, Patterson closed: "I would therefore beg leave most earnestly to recommend an increase of our present force."

"Tell General Morgan," Jackson instructed, "that . . . the main attack will be on this side, and I have no men to spare. He must maintain his position at all hazards."

Dispatching the courier with this message, he turned to the shadows of his aides.

"Gentlemen," he said, "we have slept enough."

There followed the soft sounds of belts being adjusted and pistols being replaced in their holsters.

It was shortly after one o'clock in the morning of January 8, 1815.

Followed by Lieutenant Billy Phillips leading his horse, Jackson led his small group out into the cold river fog and darkness.

Starting at the right, with the two-gun bastion that projected thirty yards out from the main line to command the levee road and the banks of the Mississippi, he walked out onto the platform to talk with the gunners for the six-pounders from the Forty-Fourth U.S. Infantry Regiment and their defenders from the Seventh U.S. Infantry.

Noting that they were holding a post of great danger, he urged them to be vigilant.

Immediately to their rear, along the main line, Beale's City Rifles extended that line out to the banks of the river.

Then Old Hickory and his party moved left along the ramparts, speaking to the troops, and checking preparations for the hell that was to come.

The next stop would be Battery Number One, under command of the cigar-smoking Regular Captain Humphrey, supported by infantry of the Seventh U.S. Regiment. Then would come Battery Number Two under U.S. Navy Lieutenant Norris, late of the USS *Carolina.*

The small party moved on to the New Orleans Volunteers of Captain Plauché, and Lacoste's battalion of Free Men of Color, followed by Daquin's Haitians.

Everywhere Jackson spoke low-voiced words of encouragement to his men; they responded with quiet enthusiasm to their straight-backed, hawk-eyed commander.

Next, the Baratarian pirates battery, where Dominique

Youx and his men were dripping coffee in the Creole way, frowned into the night.

It smelled so good in the cold river air that Jackson asked him, "You smuggle it?"

"Mebbe so, Ge'n'eral," the little captain responded, pouring him a cup.

"I wish I had five hundred such devils in the butts," Jackson told Renato Beluche, the other pirate commander.

Battery Number Four, under Lieutenant Crawley, welcomed Old Hickory next, surrounded by soldiers of the Forty-Fourth Infantry. Then Jackson spoke to Battery Number Five, under Captain Henry Perry; and Battery Number Six, under French General Garriques Flaugeac, who had commanded a division in Egypt under Napoleon.

Batteries Seven and Eight, in front of the Tennessee line commanded by General William Carroll, were served by U.S. Regulars.

In the Tennessee division Jackson addressed many of the soldiers by name, having served with them on other fields.

Then came his favorites: Tennesseans of Coffee's division, where again he could have been back in his old home neighborhood.

Here he dictated an order to Brigadier General Adair, who was acting for the ailing General Thomas, to bring up his Kentucky troops and form a two-line reserve behind the juncture of Carroll's and Coffee's troops. This point, he believed, would be the main British objective.

It was now a bitterly cold three o'clock on a morning enfolded in black velvet.

On his journey down the lines, Jackson not only had keenly observed the readiness to resist the coming assault, but he also had let his motley collection of troops see that he was with them in their time of trial.

On the long line he had approximately 5000 officers and men at their battle posts.

While the American lines were quiet with anxious waiting, for the British the hours of darkness were marked by harried, even frenzied activity.

Early in the evening forty-two boats from the fleet had been floated into the Villeré Canal, with a dam built behind them to contain the river waters when the levee had been breached. This would allow them to be floated out onto the waters of the main river.

When inspecting the work, Pakenham had asked his engineer officer, Burgoyne: "Are you satisfied the dam will bear the weight of water which will be upon it when the banks of the river are cut?"

"Perfectly," Burgoyne replied. "I should be more so if a second dam was constructed."

Then with his orders issued for the attack, Sir Edward went to bed.

This may have been his first mistake of a long evening.

While he was sleeping, the first boats were dragged through the cut in the levee at about nine o'clock. But the river was low, so a long, laborious task faced the troops in hauling the boats out of the canal and into the Mississippi.

Major Harry Smith blamed the difficulties on the collapse of the dam "as Sir Edward seemed to anticipate."

Burgoyne blamed "the banks of the new cutting" for falling into the canal.

Artillerist Dickson reported that at the barrier at the levee, the seamen labored "in a deep Mud into which they frequently sunk up to the Middle."

Even with exertions "beyond belief," only thirty of the forty-two boats were in the river by 3:15 A.M.

In all this time, no one thought to awaken the commander in chief, who slumbered on peacefully.

But there were other difficulties.

At 2:30 A.M. Sir Thomas Troubridge, who was directing the navy crews detailed to haul the heavy guns into their battery positions before the American line, reported to Dickson that the parties moving the cannon to the center batteries had been unable to find a direct route. They had been forced to go up the levee road and then inland from there.

The artillery chief sent Lieutenant Benson Earle Hill to speed up the work, only to have him report back at 4:30 that the batteries were "not half finished" and it was doubtful they could be completed by daylight.

At 4:00, under the black cloak of night and heavy river fog, the infantry columns began to move forward to their assault jump-off areas.

So when Sir Edward Pakenham rose at 5:00, he found his army in motion all around him, confronting difficulties he had not anticipated.

Dickson told his journal:

He was Surprised on learning that Col. Thornton had not yet put off, and finding it so near daylight he felt doubtful whether to let the Detachment go, as there could not be time for them to get possession of the works on the other side, and bring up Artillery to enfilade the Enemies line in Corroboration of the general attack, which was to take place at daylight, but considering that at all events Col. Thornton's attack on the other side might as a diversion greatly Assist the main attack, he sent to the boats to know the number of men on board, and having been informed in reply that the 85th were on board with Marines, making them up to 460, that there were 9 boats still to get into the river, but that those afloat would take 100 Men more, he ordered these to be embarked, and that the boats should put off, which was done accordingly.

At this stage he sent for his adjutant general, Major Harry Smith, who had been seconded to General Lambert as his military secretary.

Smith arrived to find Pakenham "greatly agitated."

He told Smith: "The dam, as you heard me say it would, gave way, and Thornton's people will be of no use whatever to the general attack."

Now he had to go with his frontal attack on Jackson's

lines, still subject to flanking fire from across the river, instead of having his own guns enfilading the American ramparts. His other option was to call off the whole operation and return to his original positions.

Smith urged him to do this.

"While we were talking, the streaks of daylight began to appear," Smith wrote later, "although the morning was dull, close and heavy, the clouds almost touching the ground."

But Pakenham refused.

"I have twice deferred the attack," he told Smith. "We are strong in numbers comparatively. It will cost more men, and the assault must be made. It is now too late."

At this point he ordered the rocket that would signal the troops to advance be fired.

35

Field of Blood

A T SIX O'CLOCK, WITH A PALE WATERY LIGHT ATTEMPTING to break through the fog and the darkness, Jackson stood on the ramparts with Generals Carroll and Adair staring into the obscurity before them. Pickets already had reported British columns forming on the trodden fields of the Chalmette plantation a mere half mile away.

His engineer, Major Latour, after noting the direction of the wind predicted that the fog would clear in an hour.

Jackson called Billy Phillips to get his telescope from the Macarty mansion.

Just then a rocket rising from the field before them, soared into the dark skies to burst in a bluish silver shower.

It was immediately answered by another rocket from the levee by the river bank.

"That is their signal for advance, I believe," Jackson said quietly.

The Battle for New Orleans had begun.

Because they were so close to the ramparts, it was vital to the British to advance and storm the American line as quickly as possible. But with the main attack to be delivered by General Gibbs's column coming up on Jackson's left, a fatal blunder already had occurred when the advance guard from the Forty-Fourth Regiment had failed to bring forward the brush fascines and the wooden ladders necessary to cross the ditch and mount the rampart walls to their front.

This failure on the part of the advance guard commander to obey his explicit orders, threw Gibbs's attack into confusion and disorder.

While Jackson stood with his generals on the rampart line, a slight breeze moved the fog away before him.

There were the British Redcoats heading straight for the point he had determined would be their objective.

Frost on the cane stubble of the Chalmette plantation had turned it into a field of silver on which the red-coated infantry with their white cross belts and glittering bayonets, and the Scottish regiment with its tartan plaided trousers, created an unforgettable picture of war.

Jackson called to Carroll and Adair to have each rifleman "aim above the cross plates" when they came within range.

One of these riflemen recalled:

> The men were tense, but very cold. The enemy was now within five hundred yards. . . . Then—boom! went our first guns . . . the long brass 12-pounder . . . commanded by Old General Fleaujeac. . . . Then all the guns opened. The British batteries . . . concealed from us by the fog replied, directing their fire by the sound of our guns . . . their flashes light up the fog . . . into all the hues of the rainbow.

When Adair shouted that the cannon smoke was spoiling the riflemen's aim, Jackson halted the fire of Batteries Seven and Eight.

Old Hickory, in his blue tunic, white breeches above black dragoon boots and his cocked hat, stood amid the swirling turmoil of the battle, openly admiring the bravery of the British charge.

Their ranks cut to pieces by artillery shell and rifle fire, the British still came on, with some of them spilling over into the ramparts manned by Adair's Kentucky troops. But they could not stay and began to drift back toward the rear.

At this critical moment a horseman spurred into the very front ranks to rally his troops. It was Major Samuel Gibbs, commander on the British right.

His efforts were in vain in the noise and confusion of repulse in front of the sheets of flame from the rifle fire of the Americans. Soon he went down, mortally wounded.

The advance against the American defenses along the levee went better for the British.

Colonel Rennie, commanding Keane's advance guard with three light companies from the Twenty-First, Forty-Third and Ninety-Third Regiments, stormed into the projecting redoubt alongside the river and drove the defenders out. They were beginning to spike the guns when they came under heavy counterattack.

The gallant colonel was shot dead after he had mounted the main American rampart line behind the redoubt, and shortly thereafter his men were driven back.

Upon the order of General Pakenham, Keane slanted his brigade across that fearful field to come to the aid of Gibbs's broken regiments. Leading the way was his Ninety-Third Regiment of Argyll and Sutherland Highlanders, in their tartan trousers, red coats and white cross belts. As they neared the rampart, they began their charge with levelled bayonets and their pipers skirling out the regimental charge music of "Monymusk" to urge them on.

Lieutenant Gordon later recorded in his diary:

> The enemy . . . no sooner got us within 150 yards of their works than a most destructive and murderous fire was opened on our Column of round, grape, musquetry, rifle, and buckshot along the whole course and length of our line

in front; as well as on our left flank. Not daunted, however, we continued our advance which in one minute would have carried us into their ditch, when we received a peremptory order to halt—this indeed was the moment of trial. The officers and men being as it were mowed down by ranks, impatient to get at the enemy at all hazards, yet compelled for want of orders to stand still and neither to advance or retire, galled as they were by this murderous fire of an invisible enemy, for a single American soldier we did not see that day, they kept discharging their musquets and rifles without lifting their faces above the ramparts.

The regiment's Colonel Robert Dale reached the foot of the American rampart expecting to find fascines in the ditch and ladders on the wall, only to discover soldiers of the Twenty-First Regiment and skirmishers from the Rifle Brigade attempting to cut steps in the face of the wall with their bayonets. While rallying his men, he was shot dead.

At the start of the battle, when he and his staff trotted past the reserve brigade, Pakenham had called out, "That's a terrific fire, Lambert."

Shortly thereafter, on seeing Gibbs's troops in trouble at the foot of the rampart, he spurred his horse into a gallop to take command, and was heard to exclaim with anger: "Lost from want of courage." While passing the Highlanders, a staff officer called out to them: "Ninety-Third! Have a little patience and you shall have your revenge."

Arriving in the heart of the melee, Pakenham rallied the men and then turned to lead them in the assault when grapeshot shattered his knee and his horse went down under him. Major Duncan Macdougall, his senior aide, dismounted to assist him to his feet, only to see the general take another bullet in his arm.

After some difficulty he was placed in the saddle of his aide's pony with Macdougall leading the horse.

In another moment he held his hat high, shouting: "Come on Brave Ninety-Third!" before being struck in the spine. He died as he was being carried to the rear.

With the high command shattered, Pakenham's new

assistant adjutant general, Sir John Tylden, rode off to the left to find General Keane. But he, too, was out of action with a bullet in the groin.

Sir John Lambert was now the ranking officer on the field. His reserve brigade was advancing into a field of bloody chaos. Halting his troops to take whatever cover they could, he went over to Gibbs's forward headquarters to confer with Admiral Cochrane, who had come onto the field. After the conference he ordered the Artillerist Dickson to cross the Mississippi to determine if Thornton had effected a lodgment on the west bank.

Hidden by heavy fog that had descended on the battlefield and the river, Dickson and Major Ord were rowed across the river to be told that Colonel Thornton and Navy Captain Money had been taken back to the British camp with severe wounds.

But Thornton had achieved victory for the British on the west bank of the river.

Landing with just 560 men and 1,000 yards below where he should have gone ashore because of an extremely strong current, he quickly had advanced against and routed a forward detachment at Mayhew's plantation. Then he continued up river against General Morgan's main position, from which Commandant Patterson had maintained effective long-range fire across the river on Pakenham's army as it had advanced against the American rampart line.

Now Patterson attempted to turn his guns on Thornton, but before he could do any damage the British overwhelmed Morgan's poorly defended right flank and advanced on the river battery and its protecting infantry.

Patterson was forced to withdraw, leaving sixteen guns in the hands of the British.

But what had been achieved by the efficient Thornton would be nullified by crossed orders and timidity.

Dickson, moving up to the scene of action, found that Major Harry Smith of Lambert's staff already had passed the orders to withdraw, and Patterson's guns were being destroyed.

Dickson stopped this, but it effectively ended any further British advance.

When he returned to Lambert to tell him the west bank could not be held by fewer than 2000 troops, Lambert ordered all troops recalled from that bank.

Earlier, Jackson, extremely upset by Morgan's defeat, sent former French General Jean Marie Humbert with 400 men to take over command from Morgan. But things would not go forward by the military book, according to Jackson's engineer, Major Latour.

> . . . there arose disputes concerning military precedence. Other militia officers did not think it right that a French general, enjoying the confidence of a large proportion of the troops; known by reputation which he had acquired, not on parade, or at reviews, but by his sword; holding a rank which he owed, not to the commission of a state governor and legislative assembly, but to which he had been raised, step by step, through all the inferior grades, and after having fought in a number of battles—these officers, I say, did not think it becoming that a French general . . . should be sent to remedy the faults of others, and repulse invaders, who, perhaps, would not, with impunity, have landed on that bank, had he there commanded. Happily, during this discussion, the enemy . . . thought it prudent to retreat.

At 8:30 the American riflemen halted all fire, although the artillery batteries continued on until around 2:00 in the afternoon.

Sometime after this Lambert dispatched Major Harry Smith across the somber field to Jackson under a flag of truce.

It would not be an easy task.

Smith wrote:

> It was a long time before I could induce them to receive me. They fired on me with cannon and musketry, which excited my choler somewhat, for a round shot tore away the ground under my right foot, which it would have been a

bore indeed to have lost under such circumstances. However, they did receive me at last and the reply from General Jackson was a very courteous one.

Jackson agreed to a temporary halt in hostilities until noon of January 9, with no reinforcements to be sent by either army to the west bank before midnight of January 9.

Asking for time to consider, Lambert finally accepted the truce terms at 10 A.M. on January 9. During the interim he had withdrawn all troops from the west bank.

The truce line was drawn 300 yards in advance of the American position, leaving 300 British wounded in their care. These men were taken to New Orleans, where they were treated kindly.

American casualties in the battle were minimal with six killed and seven wounded on the rampart. The total included seventy-one killed, wounded and missing on both banks of the river.

British losses were extremely heavy: 285 men killed, 1,186 wounded and 484 taken prisoner before the Rodriguez Canal line.

When he looked out over the bloody field covered with the red-coated bodies of the slain, Jackson fell silent.

It had been a great victory.

Then as he continued to stare after the guns went quiet, a strange movement caught his eye.

"I never had so grand and awful an idea of the resurrection," he said, "as when I saw . . . more than five hundred Britons emerging from the heaps of their dead comrades, all over the plain rising up and . . . coming forward . . . as prisoners."

Then upon learning of the great losses of the British and the small number of American dead and wounded, he declared, "The unerring hand of providence shielded my men."

36

Painful Pullout

FROM 10 A.M. UNTIL NOON ON MONDAY, JANUARY 9, BOTH armies were busy in burying the dead and removing the wounded from the bloody field. The Chalmette plantation was a ghastly mess, with British bodies strewn in all directions.

At the De la Ronde plantation the English set up their field hospital, where Surgeon Inspector General Robb and his assistants had to care for three times the number of casualties they had been warned to expect.

It was a macabre scene. Lieutenant Benson Earle Hill wrote: "Almost every room was crowded with the wounded and dying. . . . I was the unwilling spectator of numerous amputations; and on all sides nothing was heard but the piteous cries of my poor countrymen."

The bodies of Generals Pakenham and Gibbs were sealed into casks of rum for shipment to England. The pair eventually would be immortalized in a statue in St. Paul's Cathedral in London.

Keane survived the action thanks to the thickness of the clothing he was wearing during the battle.

The losses in the other officer and noncommissioned officers' ranks were appalling.

Jackson issued a message to the troops, praising them for "one of the most brilliant victories in the annals of the war."

To Secretary of War Monroe he wrote on the following day: "The enemy having concentrated his forces, may again attempt to drive me from my position by storm."

Although some of his officers, notably Hinds of the Mississippi Dragoons, urged him to leave his entrenched line and attack the British, Livingston asked: "What do you want more? The city is saved." Jackson refused to move from the rampart line.

To do so only would have accommodated the British, of whom Major Norman Pringle said, "It was the prayer of every soldier" that the Americans would attack and fight out in the open.

But in the interval the American artillery was busy shelling the British lines.

Lieutenant Gleig wrote:

> Of the extreme unpleasantness of our situation it is hardly possible to convey an adequate conception. We never closed our eyes in peace, for we were sure to be awakened before many minutes elapsed, by the splash of round shot or shell in the mud beside us. Besides all this, heavy rains now set in, accompanied with violent storms of thunder and lightning, which lasting during the entire day, usually ceased towards dark, and gave place to keen frosts. Thus we were alternately wet and frozen.

In addition there was the nightly attack on the British pickets.

> Nor were these the only evils which tended to lessen our numbers. To our soldiers every inducement was held out by

the enemy to desert. Printed papers, offering lands and money as the price for desertion, were thrown into the piquets, whilst individuals made a practice of approaching our posts, and endeavouring to persuade the very sentinels to quit their stations. . . . Many desertions began daily to take place. . . .

All the while General Lambert was preparing for a withdrawal and retreat from his most difficult position.

At about the same time the burial parties were working before the Rodriguez Canal line that Monday morning, five small British war vessels sailed up from the mouth of the Mississippi to anchor two miles below Fort St. Philip, the major American river fortress that guarded the approaches to New Orleans. While the garrison watched, the small flotilla sent two barges farther up river to take soundings close in to the fort, but these were driven off by a small gunboat commanded by United States Navy Lieutenant Thomas Cunningham, which was serving as a scout on the river.

At about 3:30 in the afternoon, the barges were followed by two British bomb craft that opened fire on the fort with four heavy mortars.

Major Walter H. Overton, commander of the fortress found to his "great mortification" that they were beyond the effective range of his twenty-nine twenty-four pounders and his two thirty-two pound cannon. For the next eight days the 366 men of the Seventh Infantry in the fort had to endure a rain of more than 1000 heavy shells. Although they did some damage to the fortress and caused a few casualties, most of the projectiles buried themselves harmlessly in the river mud.

On the first night of their attack, the British ships attempted to pass the fort with a fair wind over their sterns, but they were turned back and did not try again.

The bomb ships stopped firing at dawn of Janaury 18, whereupon all the enemy vessels sailed off not to reappear again.

During the action on January 10, Dudley Avery wrote to his mother:

The enemy have five vessels in the river below Fort Plaquemine [St. Philip] we have heard a heavy cannonade today in that direction, if they should pass that fort, all our efforts here I am afraid will be unavailing, there would be but little to prevent them after from coming to New Orleans. . . .

This enemy activity on the lower reaches of the river increased Jackson's fears of another attack. The main rampart line was strengthened further while the lines across the river were reinforced with more batteries.

While Old Hickory could think only of preparing to repel another attack, General Lambert was quietly and secretly preparing to pull his beaten army back to the ships.

Because he didn't have enough boats to move down the bayou expeditiously, he decided to build a road all the way to the mouth of the Bayou Bienvenue so he could move there by land. At the mouth he would establish a fortified base so the army could be safely ferried across Lake Borgne and out into the gulf to the anchorage off Cat Island.

To hide his intentions some troops were kept well forward in what could be used for assault positions against the American lines. Meanwhile, the rest of the British Army worked night and day on Lambert's road.

The wounded, stores and baggage and all noncombatant personnel were moved down the Mazant and Bienvenue Bayous by boat to the lake, and thence on to the ships.

A new regiment, the Fortieth, which had landed at the mouth of the bayou, was returned back to its ships.

First out from the British encampment were the First and Fifth West India Regiments, to be followed four days later by the Forty-Fourth and the marines, with the Fourteenth Light Dragoons coming along in trace.

By January 18 Lambert had seven regiments left to withdraw from his front. As soon as it was dark, the Twenty-First Regiment led the way, followed at one-hour intervals by the Fourth, Ninety-Third and Eighty-Fifth. Dickson, who was at the mouth of the bayou, had detailed Lieutenant Speer the job of spiking the six eighteen-pound cannon in the river front batteries.

Lieutenant Gleig remembered:

> Trimming the fires, and arranging all things in the same order as if no change were to take place, regiment after regiment stole away, as soon as darkness concealed their motions; leaving the piquets to follow as a rear-guard, but with strict injunctions not to retire till daylight began to appear. As may be supposed, the most profound silence was maintained; not a man opening his mouth, except to issue necessary orders, and even then speaking in a whisper. Not a cough or any other noise was to be heard from the head to the rear of the column; and even the steps of the soldiers were planted with care, to prevent the slightest stamping or echo.

Moving so many men over what only at its best could be a makeshift road quickly led to its deterioration. When the regiments in the rear of the line began their march, they had to contend with almost a mire.

Gleig wrote:

> . . . by the time the rear of the column gained the morass all trace of a way had entirely disappeared. But not only were the reeds torn asunder and sunk by the pressure of those who had gone before, but the bog itself, which at first might have furnished a few spots of firm footing, was trodden into the consistency of mud. The consequence was, that every step sank us to the knees, and frequently higher. Near the ditches, indeed, many spots occurred which we had the utmost difficulty in crossing at all. . . . At one of these places I myself beheld an unfortunate wretch gradually sink until he totally disappeared.

Gleig himself was saved from drowning in the mud when one of his men tossed him a canteen strap just as he was about to go under.

The last three regiments in the march—the Ninety-Fifth,

Forty-Third and Seventh—with the rear guard pickets took more than ten hours to cover nine miles of the quagmire road.

Last out of the Villeré encampment were General Lambert and Admiral Malcolm. They went down the bayou in a boat, followed by Colonels Dickson and Burgoyne in an armed barge of the *Asia,* with Lieutenant Peddie following last to assure the destruction of all bridges.

By January 19 the army was very uncomfortable but safe. It bivouaced in the area of the Spanish fishermen's village at the wide mouth of the Bienvenue Bayou, where the British had started their initial penetration of the New Orleans plantation area.

It would take nine days more for the boats to sail and row the rest of the troops back to their ships. On January 27 all companies of the last regiments, the Seventh and the Forty-Third, were boarding their transports in very rough seas and winds that would confine all crews to their ships for six days of gale-force weather. But by that time the retreat and withdrawal of all the army would have been completed in a professional and successful operation.

Not until dawn of January 19 did Jackson's forces realize that the British had pulled out with as much stealth and silence as they had originally filed in to the Villeré plantation in December.

Probing patrols found it to be true—the British had gone. It became official when British Surgeon General David C. Ker was taken to Jackson with a letter from Lambert in which the British general admitted that for the time the campaign had been suspended. In the letter he requested the Americans care for some eighty men too severely wounded to be moved.

Jackson ordered they be taken to hospitals in New Orleans by steamboat. Several days before, his aide Edward Livingstone had arranged with Lambert's military secretary, Major Smith, for the exchange of prisoners.

But now in the aftermath of the greatest victory of the war, Old Hickory found his worries increased.

First there were the British. He had parried and then broken their mighty thrust, but with their powerful fleet and army they were capable of striking again.

But where?

Their whole force now was back aboard the fleet, which gave them a wide-ranging capability of hitting directly at New Orleans over Lake Borgne. Or, there was always Mobile, with its magnificent bay for a base of operations.

All he could do was keep his guard up.

This was becoming more difficult daily because the citizens of New Orleans and much of the army, in celebrating the magnificent battle, had convinced themselves that all danger was past.

It was time to return to the business of trade and renew the gay life of the town that even then was famous throughout the South.

The troops were withdrawn to the city on January 21, leaving only a token force on the rampart line. On January 23 a victory parade ended at the great St. Louis Cathedral on the Place d'Armes, where a service of thanksgiving was given in praise to God and General Jackson.

That night the residents went to their beds satisfied that the long, disagreeable business of war was over. They awoke the next day to find the city under martial law.

The general placed his troops about the city ready to respond to an attack from any quarter.

Even while Jackson coped with disaffection within his own lines, the British admirals and generals were gathered in Admiral Cochrane's spacious cabin in the eighty-gun *Tonnant*, plotting their next move against him. It would not be on New Orleans—it would be on Mobile Bay.

General Lambert laid out the plans. First would come the capture of Fort Bowyer, after which an attack on the city of Mobile would be considered.

By the successful conclusion of a campaign with these limited objectives, Lambert would restore the confidence of his troops and secure an adequate land base for his forces. After that, who could know?

While the rest of the army under General Keane was landed on Dauphine Island, Lambert took the second brigade, composed of the Fourth, Twenty-First and Forty-Fourth Regiments, ashore on Mobile Point three miles east of the fort. Dickson would go over the beach next with a plentitude of heavy guns. By the morning of February 11, Engineer Burgoyne had run his siege trenches up to within twenty-five yards of the fort.

Lambert was leaving absolutely nothing to chance.

At ten o'clock he sent Major Smith forward under a flag of truce to demand surrender of the fort from its commander, Colonel William Lawrence. He asked for two hours to consider Lambert's terms.

At noon he signified he would surrender at noon the following day, at which time the garrison of 370 officers and men marched out and stacked their arms. Old Hickory's great strongpoint had gone down.

The following day, February 13, the frigate *Brazen*, out of England after a stormy voyage, signalled the flagship that she had important dispatches for the commanders in chief.

It was then the British commanders learned that a treaty of peace had been signed in the city of Ghent, Belgium, on December 24.

Jackson was infuriated by news of the loss of Fort Bowyer, which he received on February 19. On February 21 Admiral Cochrane's launch would bring him an English foreign office bulletin announcing the signing of the Treaty of Ghent.

Even to the cautious Jackson it appeared that the war was ending.

But for him the Battle of New Orleans never would end.

It would continue for the rest of his life.

Part X

. . . they crowned him with laurel. The Lord has promised his humble followers a crown that fadeth not away; the present one is already withered the leaves falling off. . . . Pray for your sister in a heathen land.
        —Rachel Jackson, New Orleans

37

Conquering Hero

THE FIRST HARBINGER OF WHAT WAS TO COME WAS THE deference paid to the General and Mrs. Jackson by New Orleans society. Rachel had come down from Nashville to join her husband in early March and received a friendly reception from the Creole ladies and their consorts.

Rachel was of a warm and lively nature. Even her rather plump figure proved no social handicap to the swirl of invitations to dinners, balls and plays that submerged the couple.

The fun-loving Creoles even persuaded them to dance at one formal ball. One New Orleans merchant noted: "To see these two figures, the general a long, haggard man, with limbs like a skeleton, and Madame le Generale, a short, fat dumpling, bobbing opposite each other . . . to the wild melody of 'Possum up de Gum Tree' . . . was very remarkable."

The couple's return to Tennessee was a triumphal procession climaxed with a great welcome at Nashville.

Major General Andrew Jackson was the most famous man in America.

He also received the thanks of the Congress before being named to command the Southern Division of the United States Army.

Retiring to their home at The Hermitage, he and Rachel were at last to get a little rest.

But it would not be for very long.

In 1817 he was ordered to suppress the Seminole Indians, who had been raiding the southern borders of the United States. But when he and his troops pursued the fleeing Indians into Spanish Florida, criticism was levelled at the fiery-tempered commanding general.

Henry Clay of Kentucky told the U.S. Senate: "It was in the provinces that were laid the seeds of the ambitious projects that overturned the liberties of Rome."

But in the end Old Hickory's action was applauded by a decisive vote.

Finally, when Spain ceded Florida to the United States in 1819 and President Monroe asked Jackson to become the territory's first governor, Old Hickory reluctantly took Rachel with him back to Pensacola.

Gossips said he was offered the office so Monroe would not have to name him commander in chief of the army.

But in less than a year the pair were back in The Hermitage and the Tennessee politicians were talking up a storm in support of the nomination of Jackson to be president of the United States.

Although at first a reluctant candidate, his fighting blood became aroused. The hero of New Orleans became a formidable figure in the campaign—so formidable that he soon became the favorite to win.

When the votes were counted in the election of 1822,

Jackson had carried Pennsylvania, the Carolinas and most of the West for a total of ninety-nine electoral votes.

John Quincy Adams of Massachusetts was second with eighty-four and William Crawford of Georgia finished third. With no candidate having a majority, the election was thrown into the House of Representatives, where Clay gave his support to Adams, who won with thirteen states to Jackson's seven.

The matter might have ended then and there, except the new president promptly named Henry Clay as his secretary of state. Immediately charges of a "corrupt bargain" filled the political air.

Jackson was enraged and just as promptly began the presidential campaign for 1828. It would be a vicious and dirty one, involving not only the good name of Jackson but also of his wife Rachel as well.

The new president, John Quincy Adams, would not have a peaceful term.

38

The Beaten

IF JACKSON WAS GOING TO BE CALLED TO OTHER AND greater fields, so were his defeated opponents in the command hierarchy of the British Army and Navy.

Resting and reviving the strength of their soldiers and seamen on Dauphine Island, just west of the Fort Bowyer peninsula across the mouth of Mobile Bay, Admiral Cochrane and General Lambert prepared to bid farewell to the Alabama coast and begin the long voyage back to England.

They began the trip home when the fleet reembarked the soldiers on March 15. They set sail for a stopover at Havana before standing out into the Atlantic.

When they reached the coast of France off Brest on May 7, the officers were surprised on looking through their long glasses to see the tricolor snapping in the breeze atop the citadel. Anchoring off Spithead on the ninth of May, they learned that Napoleon was back in the saddle after escaping from Elba on February 26.

The troops were going to have a chance to regain their reputations against their old and more familiar enemy.

Sent across the channel to meet his old foe, the Duke of Wellington complained about the state of his forces. "I have got an infamous army," he wrote, "very weak and ill-equipped, and a very inexperienced Staff."

His cries for help would bring to his side many of his veterans from his victorious Peninsular Campaign against the French in Portugal and Spain.

Major General Sir John Lambert, now commanding what had been Pakenham's army, would bring with him to the Iron Duke's side officers and men who had been with him before Old Hickory's mud ramparts at New Orleans.

There would be the artillerist, Colonel Alexander Dickson, and Colonel Francis Brooke, who led his reinforcing brigade up the Bienvenue and Mazant Bayous to assist Thornton after the British repulse at the Villeré plantation in the night battle of December 23. Major Harry Smith, who had been Sir Edward Pakenham's assistant adjutant general, would be reporting to Wellington along with the veteran Fourth, Seventh, Fortieth, Forty-Third and Forty-Fourth Regiments that had suffered so at the hands of Jackson's men in the series of Louisiana battles.

But this time they would be more successful. They defeated the French formations under Napoleon at Waterloo on June 18, 1815.

Lambert would retire with the rank of general after years of service.

John Keane would continue in the service and command the army of the Indus and storm Ghuznee and Kabul in 1839.

The redoubtable Colonel Thornton would be knighted and become a lieutenant general, only to shoot himself in 1840 because of his wounds.

Harry Smith would become a major general after service

in South Africa and India, while his beautiful wife would be immortalized in the name of the town of Ladysmith, Natal, South Africa.

Sir Alexander Cochrane, naval commander in chief on the American station, and maybe the evil genius for the British in the New Orleans campaign, would be promoted in the Order of the Bath to Knight Grand Cross in 1815 and from vice admiral to admiral in 1819.

Both Admiral Codrington, Cochrane's chief of staff, and Admiral Pulteney Malcolm, in charge of support functions, would be knighted in 1815. Codrington would command the allied fleet that sank the Turkish fleet at the Battle of Navarino in 1827.

The great allied victory at Waterloo, coming so close on the heels of the Battle of New Orleans, dimmed English memories of the catastrophe of British arms before Jackson's ramparts. New Orleans came to be an almost unremembered battle.

This would not be so in the United States, where it became the "only" land battle of the War of 1812. It's fame resounded from one end of the country to the other—no matter that it technically took place after the treaty of peace had been signed.

It proved that there was at least one American general who could outplan, outthink, and out-act the pick of Britain's military and naval commanders.

It bolstered the self-pride of the new nation, and in so doing catapulted Andrew Jackson into the very forefront of American heroes.

This alone would ensure that the effects of the Battle of New Orleans would reverberate throughout the history of the United States—even until the present day.

39

Political Cockpit

G EORGE WASHINGTON. JOHN ADAMS. THOMAS JEFFERSON.
James Madison. James Monroe.

The list of past presidents was a litany of Revolutionary
War history.

Now came John Quincy Adams, son of the second president but with few other ties to the war years. There had
been a distinct break with the past.

He would be facing a most formidable opponent in
Andrew Jackson over the next four years of his administration. Jackson did have direct ties with the revolution and
scars to prove it. He also was the personification of American resistance to Great Britain in the Second War for
Independence of 1812.

Where Old Hickory had been a reluctant candidate at
the start of the campaign of 1822, the frontier perception

that the election had been stolen from him by the vote in the House of Representatives guaranteed that contention for the 1828 election would be relentless and vindictive.

It also would be regarded, rightly or wrongly, as the entrenched money power of the East against the "common man" agrarian interests of the South and West.

Also for the first time, the nominations would be made by legislatures or mass meetings instead of the traditional congressional caucuses.

The old one-party system would split in two, with Adams and Clay running as National Republicans (later to become Whigs), and the Jacksonians as the Democratic Republicans (later to become simply the Democrats).

It would be a savage campaign.

Adams claimed that Jackson had no program to offer the people.

Jackson retorted that the Adams program was to thwart the will of the people. It would be aristocracy versus democracy.

From these beginnings the rhetoric took off. It would be passionate and lurid.

Jackson would be labelled a murderer, duelist, gambler, swearer, cock fighter, conspirator with Aaron Burr, brawler, and finally an adulterer—this last with reference to his double marriage to Rachel Robards-Jackson. This charge would make Jackson the lifelong enemy of John Quincy Adams.

Adams would be attacked as a monarchist, aristocrat, and representative of the hated "money power" of the East.

In the end it would be "no contest."

Jackson would defeat Adams by capturing New York and Pennsylvania, along with the Southern and Western states, for 178 electoral votes. Adams received eighty-three electoral votes. Calhoun would be the vice president.

But the victory would have a tragic end.

While preparing for the long trip from The Hermitage to the White House, Rachel Jackson, suffering from a heart ailment complicated by excess weight, would complain that she was feeling faint. For three days it seemed that her condition was improving.

The general and the doctors kept watch in adjoining rooms when suddenly she suffered a sharp attack. Jackson and the doctors got to her side, but it was too late.

Rachel was dead.

She was buried the day before Christmas in the garden of The Hermitage.

A weeping Jackson would face the long road to Washington alone.

On January 18, 1829, after standing at her grave for a long time, he went down to The Hermitage's landing to board a steamboat for the trip down the Cumberland River on the first stage of his journey.

Washington hardly knew what to expect.

40

White House Bedlam

THE SUN SHONE BRIGHTLY ON THE PATCHES OF SNOW DOT-ting the great lawn in front of the Capitol that Inauguration Day of March 4, 1829, when General Andrew Jackson was sworn in as the seventh president of the United States.

The great crowd gathered for the ceremonies itself was a reflection of those who had rallied to his standard for the defense of New Orleans fourteen years before. Many hailed from the western states of Tennessee, Kentucky, Mississippi, Louisiana and Missouri.

Frontiersmen, backwoodsmen, farmers, and from the older states small shopkeepers, laborers and mechanics all were there. The "common people" paid their respects as "their president" took his oath of office.

Many of those who came, including veterans of the war, sought offices for themselves.

There were, of course, many representatives of the older and more staid orders of the longer established states of New England, the Middle Atlantic seaboard and the South.

But the day would belong to the common people who had brought Old Hickory to victory at the polls, just as they had brought him to victory over the British aristocrats commanding the Redcoats and seamen before New Orleans so many years before.

They would sully their day of triumph, however, with inexcusable behavior at the White House reception that followed the ceremonies.

Refusing to leave at the conclusion of the inauguration, the vast crowd streamed after the general as he rode his horse down broad Pennsylvania Avenue to his new home, which had been prepared with tables arrayed with choice viands and drink for the invited congressmen, their wives and officials of the government.

The crowd became a mob and surged into the White House to raid the waiting tables. They besieged the new president, who had to be protected by a wall of his close friends who saved him from the crush.

That night he was taken to a hotel to escape his well-wishers.

It seemed that all the fears of the conservatives had been confirmed.

Daniel Webster of Massachusetts had written to New England: "His friends have no common principle, they are held together by no common tie."

Congressman John Randolph of Roanoke went even farther: "The country is ruined past redemption; it is ruined in the spirit and character of the people. There is an abjectness of spirit that appalls and disgusts me. Where now could we find leaders of a revolution?"

Followers of the old Federalist precepts of Alexander

Hamilton would remember that he had told the delegates to the Constitutional Convention in 1787:

> All communities divide themselves into few and the many. The first are rich and well-born, the other the mass of the people. . . . The people are turbulent and changing; they seldom judge or determine right. . . . Give, therefore, to the first class a distinct, permanent share in the government. They will check the unsteadiness of the second, and, as they cannot receive any advantage by a change, they therefore will ever maintain good government.

Daniel Webster told the Massachusetts' convention:

> Power naturally and necessarily follows property. . . . A republican form of government rests not more on political constitutions than on those laws which regulate the descent and transmission of property. . . . It would seem then to be the part of political wisdom to found government on property; and to establish such distribution of property, by the laws which regulate its transmission and alienation, as to interest the great majority of society in the protection of the government.

In 1823, while he was serving Tennessee in the Senate, Jackson had taken direct issue with the premises of Federalism when he said: "I am one of those who do not believe that a national debt is a national blessing, but rather a curse to a republic; inasmuch as it is calculated to raise about the administration a moneyed aristocracy dangerous to the liberties of the country."

So as the straight-backed, fierce-eyed, haggard-faced man rode down the broad reaches of Pennsylvania Avenue to the chaotic proceedings in the White House, he little knew that he had left one great battle behind to confront two more that would be more difficult to resolve than his great victory over the British military and naval aristocracy before the Mud Rampart Line at the Battle of New Orleans.

Part XI

Our Union: It must be preserved!
 —Toast by President Jackson, April 13, 1830

41

Stormy Weather

WITH THE "COMMON MAN" SHOUTING FOR REFORM OF the administration left by John Quincy Adams, Jackson moved quickly on a secondary front to provide a highly visible answer.

The long-entrenched federal bureaucracy had for years lorded itself above the common people, serving either itself or the lords and masters of power and prestige.

Jackson's answer was to turn out the office holders and replace them with men loyal to the principles of Jacksonian democracy.

The action was to become known as the "Spoils System," after a declaration of Senator William Marcy of New York, who once stated that the politicians of his state see "nothing wrong in the rule that to the victor belong the spoils. . . ."

Jackson told Congress that "Office is considered as a species of property, and government [more] as a means of promoting individual interests than as an instrument created solely for the service of the people." He stated that the government would no longer be "an engine for the support of the few at the expense of the many."

Immediately a howl went up from Adams' National Republican followers, but to no use. The rotation-in-office policy went into effect.

But this issue of itself would be dwarfed by two others that would come to dominate the new president's administration: the Doctrine of States Rights and the future of the Second Bank of the United States.

In meeting the controversies surrounding both of these issues, Jackson would be taking on the governing aristocracies of the southern plantation states and their slaveholding constituencies in the first and the financial establishments of New England and the Middle Atlantic states in the second.

It would be quite a battle.

A complicating factor would be that Jackson's vice president, John C. Calhoun of South Carolina, spokesman for the states rights groups, wanted to be president himself.

On the bank issue his major opponent would be Nicholas Biddle, president of the Bank of the United States, who considered himself the equal if not greater than the president of the United States.

The States Rights issue came to an early head at a Jefferson Day dinner on April 13, 1830. Twenty-four toasts in support of South Carolina, which had declared it was considering nullification of federal tariff laws, were given preceding that of the President of the United States.

Jackson rose slowly, then looking directly at Calhoun raised his glass.

His toast had all the effect of artillery fire.

"Our Union: It must be preserved!"

Taken aback, Calhoun, his hand trembling so the wine

spilled over the side of his glass, then rose to respond to his chief.

"The Union, next to our liberty, most dear."

The terrible forces that would tear apart the nation thirty years later already were on the prowl.

Jackson's unequivocal stand for the Union sent shock waves through the States' Rights slaveholding states of the South.

This was so because it had been preceded earlier in the year by one of the greatest debates ever to rock the Senate of the United States.

42

Firebell in the Night

THE OPENING ROUND OF THE GREAT CONFLICT OVER THE future of slavery in the United States had come much earlier, in 1820, when the so-called "Missouri Comprise" became law. It provided that Missouri would be admitted to the Union as a slave state while Maine would enter as a free one, so keeping the then balance of power: a dozen states on each side.

Nobody had liked the compromise. John Quincy Adams called it "A title page to a great tragic volume." But on the other hand no one had any stomach for the alternative of civil war.

Former President Thomas Jefferson viewed the turmoil from his peaceful retreat at Monticello, high in the wooded uplands of Virginia. He termed the angry discord "the ugly sound of a firebell in the night."

A firebell it was, clanging its way through the 1820s,

with heightened controversy forcing the slaveholding states to seek safeguards for the assured continuance of their "peculiar institution" into the future of the new nation.

It was not going to be an easy task, for the moral issues involved in slavery were beginning to tear at the very social fabric of both North and South.

In self-defense the South had begun to settle on the self-evident claim of the sovereignty of each individual state. Each state had joined the Union of its own free will, and of its own free will it could depart.

The controversy boiled over onto the floor of the Senate most unexpectedly and with terrible heat while that body was considering the disposal of public lands in January 1830.

The argument took a sharp turn, however, when the young senator from South Carolina, Robert Hayne, shifted it to the propriety of the federal government imposing unwanted tariff restrictions on the states to the advantage of some while inflicting injury on others.

Immediately intense, stern-jawed Vice President John C. Calhoun leaned forward stiffly from his presiding officer's chair to focus all his attention on his colleague from South Carolina. Hayne was giving voice to his own contention that any state could suspend a federal law that it regarded as unconstitutional, until three-quarters of the states had justified the law through the amending power.

Another who sat up with new interest in the speaker was the senator from Massachusetts, the famous debater Daniel Webster.

No mean orator himself, Hayne launched into a diatribe on what he called the "consolidation" of powers of the federal government to the detriment of the individual states. The public lands bill, he argued, would only give additional powers to a central government that already was too powerful.

This rankled Webster, who took the floor the next day to voice his contempt for the argument.

"Consolidation, that perpetual cry both of terror and

delusion. . . . The union of the States will be strengthened by whatever furnishes inducements to the people . . . to hold together." This was no time, he told Hayne, "to calculate the value of the Union."

All the while Jackson's vice president squirmed in frustration on his bench, unable to take part in the floor fight because of his duties as presiding officer of the Senate.

The handsome South Carolinian Hayne replied to Webster that his words had angered him and he wished to return the shot.

Webster rose to fold his arms across his broad chest.

"Go ahead," he said, "I am ready to receive it."

Hayne then protested that he was defending both South Carolina and the Union by outlining a constitutional means of disagreement with the central authority by way of nullification. Otherwise, he said, a simple numerical majority, holding other views, could reduce the South to ruin.

"Who then are the friends of the Union?" Hayne asked.

He gazed into the faces of the listening senators before answering.

"Those who would confine the Federal Government strictly within the limits prescribed by the constitution. . . . And who are its enemies? Those who are in favor of consolidation; who are constantly stealing power from the States, and adding strength to the Federal Government."

All Washington waited to hear Webster deliver his answer the next day.

Galleries were overflowing with bonneted ladies and their escorts when the senator from Massachusetts took the floor to respond to the attack from the South.

Dressed in somber clothes, he addressed his remarks to his chief adversary, the silent Calhoun.

With his deep voice resounding throughout the crowded chamber, he told his listeners that the national government was not merely the creation of the states but rather that of the people themselves.

"It is, sir," he told Calhoun, "the people's Constitution,

the people's government, made for the people, made by the people, and answerable to the people."

As he spoke, his listeners were aware that they were hearing one of the greatest discourses ever delivered on the nature and meaning of the United States of America.

With the rapt attention of all, he turned directly to Calhoun:

> I profess, Sir, in my career hitherto, to have kept steadily in view the preservation of our Federal Union. It is to that Union we owe our safety at home, and our dignity abroad. It has been to us all a copious fountain of national, social, and personal happiness. I have not allowed myself, Sir, to look beyond the Union, to see what might lie hidden in the dark recess behind. While the Union lasts we have high, exciting, gratifying prospects spread out before us, for us, and our children. Beyond that I seek not to penetrate the veil.
>
> When my eyes, shall be turned to behold for the last time the sun in heaven, may I not see him shining on the broken and dishonored fragments of a once glorious Union. Let their last feeble glance rather behold the gorgeous ensign of the republic, now known and honored throughout the earth, still full high advanced, not a stripe erased or polluted, nor a single star obscured, bearing for its motto, no such miserable interrogatory as "What is all this worth?" nor those other words of delusion and folly, "Liberty first and Union afterwards," but everywhere, spread all over in characters of living light, blazing on all its ample folds, as they float over the sea and over the land, and in every wind the whole heavens, that other sentiment, dear to every true American heart—Liberty and Union, now and forever, one and inseparable!

With these jeweled words the great senator from Massachusetts rested his case.

The old general in the White House must have given his silent applause.

But the great debate was just gathering steam.

On July 26, 1831, Calhoun, while still vice president,

issued a declaration from his home in South Carolina that nullification was both a peaceable and constitutional method of dissent; that the Constitution was but an agreement between the various states and each of them was free to interpret it in its own way.

In December Jackson held out the olive branch with a reduced tariffs bill, which Congress enacted in July 1832.

But this was not enough.

That fall a special state convention meeting at Columbia, South Carolina, passed a law nullifying the federal tariff acts of 1828 and 1832 and forbidding the collection of duties within the state.

The legislature then met to vote for the raising of a state army.

It was to be war.

43

The Union Preserved

JACKSON'S HAND WAS STRENGTHENED IMMENSELY ON NO-
vember 6 when he was reelected to the presidency over
Henry Clay of Kentucky by a popular vote of 688,242 to
473,462, followed by an electoral vote of 219 to 49. Martin
Van Buren of New York would be the new vice president,
replacing Calhoun, who resigned to become a senator
from South Carolina.

The common people had spoken again.

But the conservative elements of the nation, both in the
North and in the South, saw ruin ahead.

The Boston Courier declared:

> Yet there is one comfort left: God has promised that the
> days of the wicked shall be short; the wicked is old and
> feeble, and he may die before he can be elected. It is the
> duty of every good Christian to pray to our Maker to have

pity on us. . . . We are constrained to acknowledge that the experiment of an absolutely liberal government has failed. . . Heaven be praised that Massachusetts and Connecticut have escaped the moral and political contagion! As for the rest, they have proved themselves slaves, born to be commanded—they have put the whip into the hands of one who has shown every inclination to be absolute master, and it is some consolation to think that he will probably ere long lay it upon their backs till they howl again. . . . Who doubts that if all who are unable to read or write had been excluded from the polls, Andrew Jackson could not have been elected?

When news of South Carolina's nullification ordinance reached Washington, it inflamed Old Hickory. He threatened to "hang every leader . . . of that infatuated people, sir, by martial law, irrespective of his name, or political or social position."

There was no doubt in the minds of many that he was including former Vice President John C. Calhoun in the threat.

This prompted Senator Thomas Hart Benton of Missouri to remark, "When Jackson begins to talk about hanging, they can begin to look for the ropes."

The ordinances not only declared the state would not be bound by the law, but it also forbade federal officers from collecting any import duties in South Carolina after February 1, 1833.

It concluded by warning the United States that if it tried to use force, South Carolina would secede from the Union.

Taking the rebellious citizens of the Palmetto State at their word, Jackson ordered five thousand muskets sent to Castle Pinckney in Charleston harbor along with a sloop of war and five revenue cutters. He asked the secretary of war to check on the readiness of the army to take the field and sent a secret agent to Charleston to keep him advised of developments.

On December 10 he issued the greatest of all his state papers: The Proclamation to the People of South Carolina.

The Constitution . . . forms a government, not a league. . . . It is a Government in which all the people are represented, which operates directly on the people individually, not upon the States; they retained all the power they did not grant. But each State, having expressly parted with so many powers as to constitute, jointly with the other States, a single nation, can not, from that period, possess any right to secede, because such secession does not break a league, but destroys the unity of a nation; and any injury to the unity is not only a breach which would result from the contravention of a compact, but it is an offense against the whole Union. To say that any State may at pleasure secede from the Union is to say that the United States are not a nation. . . .

In warning the citizens of South Carolina against secession, Jackson made this declaration.

But the dictates of a high duty oblige me solemnly to announce that you can not succeed. The laws of the United States must be executed. I have no discretionary power on the subject; my duty is emphatically pronounced in the Constitution. Those who told you that you might peaceably prevent their execution deceived you; they would not have been deceived themselves. They know that a forcible opposition could alone prevent the execution of the laws, and they know that such opposition must be repelled. Their object is disunion. But be not deceived by names. Disunion by armed force is treason. Are you really ready to incur its guilt; If you are, on the heads of the instigators of the act be the dreadful consequences; on their heads be the dishonor, but on yours may fall the punishment. On your unhappy State will inevitably fall all the evils of the conflict you force upon the Government of your country. It can not accede to the mad project of disunion, of which you would be the first victims. Its First Magistrate can not, if he would, avoid the performance of his duty. The consequence must be fearful for you, distressing to your fellow-citizens here and to the friends of good government throughout the world. Its enemies have beheld our prosperity with a vexation they could not conceal; it was a standing refutation of their slavish doctrines, and they will point to our discord with the triumph of malignant joy. It is yet in your power to disappoint them. . . .

Having the fullest confidence in the justness of the legal and constitutional opinion of my duties which has been expressed, I rely with equal confidence on your undivided support in my determination to execute the laws, to preserve the Union by all constitutional means, to arrest, if possible, by moderate and firm measures the necessity of a recourse to force; and if it be the will of Heaven that the recurrence of its primeval curse on man for the shedding of a brothers blood should fall upon our land, that it be not called down by any offensive act on the part of the United States. . . .

May the Great Ruler of Nations grant that the signal blessing with which He has favored ours may not, by the madness of party or personal ambition, be disregarded and lost; and may His wise providence bring those who have produced this crisis to see the folly before they feel the misery of civil strife, and inspire a returning veneration for that Union which, if we may dare to penetrate His designs, He has chosen as the only means of attaining the high destinies to which we may reasonably aspire.

—Andrew Jackson

But Charleston would not listen.

By the beginning of 1833, John Calhoun was senator from South Carolina and Robert Hayne was governor.

The stage was set.

It would be force against force. But hotheaded though they were, the South Carolinians never could forget they were facing another hothead, the old soldier, the victor of New Orleans.

Inspired by Jackson's words, the rest of the country went on a patriotic binge in support of the Union.

This made it all the more difficult for Calhoun, who rose in the Senate on January 16 to oppose Jackson's Force Bill that called for arms to put down rebellion in South Carolina. On January 22 he introduced resolutions declaring that the federal system joined "free and independent

States in a bond of union for mutual advantages" that could be preserved in either of two ways—"by the consent of its members or by a government of the sword."

On February 15 in a two-day diatribe, he called the Force Bill a measure for war.

This was too much for Daniel Webster, who answered the South Carolinian in a four-hour speech.

The Constitution, he declared, was no compact between sovereign states who might withdraw from it, but an executed contract for a permanent government of the people.

"The people of the United States are one people," he said. "They are one in making war, and one in making peace; they are one in regulating commerce, and one in laying duties."

"What, then, do the gentlemen wish?" Webster asked. "Do they wish to establish a minority government?"

The debate droned on, but Jackson was moving. If it was to be war, he would make war.

Confronted with an unyielding Jackson, Calhoun was looking into an abyss of darkness and destruction. There was no doubt about it, the old man in the White House meant war.

No one quite knows what happened, but Henry Clay, the great compromiser, came up with a way. He substituted his own tariff bill for that of the administration. Calhoun gave it his blessing and the fight was over.

Jackson had won.

Calhoun still had a wild journey to make back to South Carolina to cool off his rebels. Finally they settled for nullifying Jackson's Force Bill.

Back at his home in the pillared plantation mansion known as "Fort Hill", the exhausted intense-faced senator, looked into the future and wrote:

"The struggle, so far from being over, is not more than fairly commenced."

Part XII

The bank is trying to kill me, but I will kill it!
—Jackson to Van Buren, July 3, 1832

44

Blessing or Curse?

THE SECOND BANK OF THE UNITED STATES HAD BEEN chartered as a privately owned and controlled institution in 1816. Located in Philadelphia, it enjoyed a special relationship with the United States government in that it was used by the Treasury Department for the deposit of the nation's money. Of its capital of $35,000,000, the United States had subscribed one-fifth of the amount. The public funds on deposit with the bank could be used for its own purposes without payment of interest, and it could issue bank notes in its name.

The states could levy no tax on it and no like financial institution was to be chartered by Congress.

In return the bank paid the United States a bonus of $1,500,000, transferred public monies and made public payments without charge, and reserved five of the twenty-five directors' seats for government appointees. The secretary of the Treasury could withdraw the government deposits only after he had given reasons for his action to Congress.

Its current charter would expire in 1836, when it would have to be renewed by action of Congress.

Nicholas Biddle, president of the bank, was the scion of an aristocratic Pennsylvania family. After serving as secretary of the American legation at the Court of St. James in London, he joined the bank as director at the insistence of President James Monroe before becoming its chief officer in 1823.

A polished, urbane gentleman who had moved in the court circles of Europe, he was a quite different man from the hard-driving, outspoken old soldier who now occupied the White House.

In 1829, after his inauguration, Jackson told him, "I do not dislike your Bank any more than all banks."

Biddle knew he had an adversary, but he had powerful friends.

Jackson had served fair notice on his opponent in his Second Annual Message of December 6, 1830, when he told the people:

The importance of the principles involved in the inquiry whether it will be proper to recharter the Bank of the United States requires that I should again call the attention of Congress to the subject. Nothing has occurred to lessen in any degree the dangers which many of our citizens apprehend from that institution as at present organized. In the spirit of improvement and compromise which distinguishes our country and its institutions it becomes us to inquire whether it be not possible to secure the advantages afforded by the present bank through the agency of a Bank of the United States so modified in its principles and structure as to obviate constitutional and other objections.

"It is thought practicable to organize such a bank with the necessary officers as a branch of the Treasury Department, based on the public and individual deposits, without power to make loans or purchase property, which shall remit the funds of the Government, and the expense of which may be paid, if thought advisable, by allowing its officers to sell bills of exchange to private individuals at a moderate premium. Not being a corporate body, having no stockholders, debtors, or property, and but few officers, it would not be obnoxious to the constitutional objections which are urged against the present bank; and having no means to operate on the hopes, fears, or interests of large masses of the community, it would be shorn of the influence which makes that bank formidable, The States would be strengthened by having in their hands the means of furnishing the local paper currency through their own banks, while the Bank of the United States, though issuing no paper, would check the issues of the State banks by taking their notes in deposit and for exchange only so long as they continue to be redeemed with specie. In times of public emergency the capacities of such an institution might be enlarged by legislative provisions.

These suggestions are made not so much as a recommendation as with a view of calling the attention of Congress to the possible modifications of a system which can not continue to exist in its present form without occasional collisions with the local authorities and perpetual apprehensions and discontent on the part of the States and the people.

Biddle, although upset by Jackson's seeming intractability, still was not convinced that now was the time to bring the issue to a head. It was his ally, Henry Clay, who convinced him otherwise.

Clay, who was preparing to head the National Republican ticket against Jackson's Democrats in the election of 1832, saw the bank issue as a major point of attack on Old Hickory in the coming campaign and persuaded Biddle that now was his best chance.

On January 9, 1832, bills providing for the rechartering of the bank were entered before both the House and the Senate.

There was going to be a fight.

45

Veto

WHILE THE BANK CONFLICT SIMMERED ITS WAY THROUGH Congress during the winter and into the spring, it came to a full boil in May.

Biddle, with the help of Clay and Webster in the Senate and John Quincy Adams in the House along with other conservatives, came to see that he held victory in his hand.

This only fueled his arrogance, which was widely known. In years past, when one of his bank officers in Washington advised him: "As . . . there are other interests to be attended to [besides those of the bank], especially that of the Government, I have deemed it proper to see and consult with the President."

Biddle set him straight by return mail.

If . . . you think that there are other interests to be attended to besides those with which you are charged by the

administration of the bank, we deem it right to correct what
is a total misapprehension. . . . The moment this appointment [of the five government directors] takes place the
Executive has completely fulfilled its functions. The entire
responsibility is thenceforward in the directors, and no
officer of the Government, from the President downwards,
has the least right, the least authority, the least pretence, for
interference in the concerns of the bank. . . . This invoca-
tion of the Government, therefore. . . . is totally inconsist-
ent with the temper and spirit which belong to the officers
of the bank, who should regard only the rights of the bank
and the instructions of those who govern it, and who
should be at all times prepared to execute the orders of the
board, in direct opposition, if need be, to the personal
interests and wishes of the President and every officer of
the Government.

Again he boasted, "I have been for years in the daily
exercise of more personal authority than any President
habitually enjoys."

Admitting he could destroy state banks and throw the
country into a depression, he declared: "Nothing but the
evidence of suffering . . . will produce any effect in Congress."

Seduced by the powers of the bank to grant or withhold
loans, he again declared, "I can remove all the constitutional scruples in the District of Columbia."

Biddle took personal charge of the legislative battle in
both houses, staunchly supported by his blue-ribbon team
of leading statesmen in Clay, Webster, Adams and George
McDuffie of South Carolina.

Who could dispute him when he said "We shall crush
the Kitchen Cabinet."

This last reference was to the informal "brain trust"
Jackson had gathered about him for determining high policy.

As expected the recharter bill passed the Senate on June
11 by a margin of twenty-eight ayes to twenty nos.

On July 3, when it passed the House by a vote of 107 to

eighty-five, Biddle came on to the floor. The members crowded about him to congratulate him on his great victory.

The triumphal party then adjourned to Biddle's quarters, where it roared on through most of the night.

Jackson received the bill on the Fourth of July.

His vice presidential running mate to be, learning of the bill's passage, hurried to Washington and the White House where he found a sick, pale president in bed.

Taking his friend's hand, Old Hickory said in a quiet solemn voice: "The bank, Mr. Van Buren, is trying to kill me, but I will kill it!"

The next day he had members of his Kitchen Cabinet hard at work perfecting a veto message.

Working night and day, their message slowly evolved from the drafting table. Jackson's advisors Amos Kendall, Roger B. Taney, Andrew Donelson and Levi Woodbury put it together while the old general, his battle blood rising, stalked in and out of the room to change a word here or a phrase there.

There would be no compromises. When it exploded on the floor of the Senate, its words would reverberate to all corners of the Union. It would be called by some the most important presidential veto in American history.

The Veto of the Bank Bill
July 10, 1832

To the Senate:

The bill "to modify and continue" the act entitled "An act to incorporate the subscribers to the Bank of the United States" was presented to me on the 4th July instant. Having considered it with that solemn regard to the principles of the Constitution which the day was calculated to inspire, and come to the conclusion that it ought not to become a law, I herewith return it to the Senate, in which it originated, with my objections.

A bank of the United States is in many respects convenient for the Government and useful to the people. Entertaining this opinion, and deeply impressed with the belief that some of the powers and privileges possessed by the existing bank are unauthorized by the Constitution, subversive of the rights of the States, and dangerous to the liberties of the people, I felt it my duty at an early period of my Administration to call the attention of Congress to the practicability of organizing an institution combining all its advantages and obviating these objections. I sincerely regret that in the act before me I can perceive none of those modifications of the bank charter which are necessary, in my opinion, to make it compatible with justice, with sound policy, or with the Constitution of our country.

The present corporate body, denominated the president, directors, and company of the Bank of the United States, will have existed at the time this act is intended to take effect twenty years. It enjoys an exclusive privilege of banking under the authority of the General Government, a monopoly of its favor and support, and, as a necessary consequence, almost a monopoly of the foreign and domestic exchange. The powers, privileges, and favors bestowed upon it in the original charter, by increasing the value of the stock far above its par value, operated as a gratuity of many millions to the stockholders. . . .

The act before me proposes another gratuity to the holders of the same stock, and in many cases to the same men, of at least seven millions more. . . . On all hands it is conceded that its passage will increase at least 20 or 30 per cent more the market price of the stock, subject to the payment of the annuity of $200,000 per year secured by the act, thus adding in a moment one-fourth to its par value. It is not our own citizens only who are to receive the bounty of our Government. More than eight millions of the stock of this bank are held by foreigners. By this act the American Republic proposes virtually to make them a present of some millions of dollars. For these gratuities to foreigners and to some of our own opulent citizens the act secures no equivalent whatever. . . .

Every monopoly and all exclusive privileges are granted at the expense of the public, which ought to receive a fair equivalent. The many millions which this act proposes to bestow on the stockholders of the existing bank must come directly or indirectly out of the earnings of the American people. It is due to them, therefore, if their Government sell monopolies and exclusive privileges, that they should at least exact for them as much as they are worth in open market. The value of the monopoly in this case may be correctly ascertained. The twenty-eight millions of stock would probably be at an advance of 50 per cent, and command in market at least $42,000,000, subject to the payment of the present bonus. The present value of the monopoly, therefore, is $17,000,000, and this the act proposes to sell for three millions, payable in fifteen annual installments of $200,000 each.

It is not conceivable how the present stockholders can have any claim to the special favor of the Government. The present corporation has enjoyed its monopoly during the period stipulated in the original contract. If we must have such a corporation, why should not the Government sell out the whole stock and thus secure to the people the full market value of the privileges granted? Why should not Congress create and sell twenty-eight millions of stock, incorporating the purchasers with all the powers and privileges secured in this act and putting the premium upon the sales into the Treasury?

But this act does not permit competition in the purchase of this monopoly. It seems to be predicated on the erroneous idea that the present stockholders have a prescriptive right not only to the favor but to the bounty of Government. It appears that more than a fourth part of the stock is held by foreigners and the residue is held by a few hundred of our own citizens, chiefly of the richest class. . . .

If our Government must sell monopolies, it would seem to be its duty to take nothing less than their full value, and if gratuities must be made once in fifteen or twenty years let them not be bestowed on the subjects of a foreign government nor upon a designated and favored class of men in our own country. It is but justice and good policy, as far as the nature of the case will admit, to confine our favors to our own fellow citizens, and let each in his turn enjoy an opportunity to profit by our bounty. In the bearings of the act before me upon these points I find ample reasons why it should not become a law. . . .

The modifications of the existing charter proposed by this act are not such, in my view, as make it consistent with the rights of the States or the liberties of the people. The qualification of the right of the bank to hold real estate, the limitation of its power to establish branches, and the power reserved to Congress to forbid the circulation of small notes are restrictions comparatively of little value or importance. All the objectionable principles of the existing corporation, and most of its odious features, are retained without alleviation. . . .

Is there no danger to our liberty and independence in a bank that in its nature has so little to bind it to our country? The president of the bank has told us that most of the State banks exist by its forbearance. Should its influence become concentered, as it may under the operation of such an act as this, in the hands of a self-elected directory, whose interests are identified with those of the foreign stockholders, will there not be cause to tremble for the purity of our elections in peace and for the independence of our country in war? Their power would be great whenever they might choose to exert it; but if this monopoly were regularly renewed every fifteen or twenty years on terms proposed by themselves, they might seldom in peace put forth their strength to influence elections or control the affairs of the nation. But if any private citizen or public functionary should interpose to curtail its powers or prevent a renewal of its privileges, it can not be doubted that he would be made to feel its influence.

Should the stock of the bank principally pass into the hands of the subjects of a foreign country, and we should unfortunately become involved in a war with that country, what would be our condition? Of the course which would be pursued by a bank almost wholly owned by the subjects of a foreign power, and managed by those whose interests, if not affections, would run in the same direction there can be no doubt. All its operation within would be in aid of the hostile fleets and armies without. Controlling our currency, receiving our public moneys, and holding thousands of our citizens in dependence, it would be more formidable and dangerous than the naval and military power of the enemy.

If we must have a bank with private stockholders, every

consideration of sound policy and every impulse of American feeling admonishes that it should be purely American. Its stockholders should be composed exclusively of our own citizens, who at least ought to be friendly to our Government and willing to support it in times of difficulty and danger.

It is maintained by the advocates of the bank that its constitutionality in all its features ought to be considered as settled by precedent and by the decision of the Supreme Court. To this conclusion I can not assent. Mere precedent is a dangerous source of authority, and should not be regarded as deciding questions of constitutional power except where the acquiescence of the people and the States can be considered as well settled. So far from this being the case on this subject, an argument against the bank might be based on precedent. One Congress, in 1791, decided in favor of a bank; another, in 1811, decided against it. One Congress in 1815, decided against a bank; another in 1816, decided in its favor. Prior to the present Congress, therefore, the prececents drawn from that source were equal. If we resort to the States, the expressions of legislative, judicial, and executive opinions against the bank have been probably to those in its favor as 4 to 1. There is nothing in precedent, therefore, which, if its authority were admitted, ought to weigh in favor of the act before me.

If the opinion of the Supreme Court covered the whole ground of this act, it ought not to control the coordinate authorities of this Government. The Congress, the Executive and the Court must each for itself be guided by its own opinion of the Constitution. Each public officer who takes an oath to support the Constitution swears that he will support it as he understands it, and not as it is understood by others. It is as much the duty of the House of Representatives, of the Senate, and of the President to decide upon the constitutionality of any bill or resolution which may be presented to them for passage or approval as it is of the supreme judges when it may be brought before them for judicial decision. The opinion of the judges has no more authority over Congress than the opinion of Congress has over the judges, and on that point the President is independent of both. The authority of the Supreme Court must not, therefore, be permitted to control the Congress or the Executive when acting in their legislative capacities, but to have only such influence as the force of their reasoning may deserve.

But in the case relied upon the Supreme Court have not decided that all the features of this corporation are compatible with the Constitution. It is true that the court have said that the law incorporating the bank is a constitutional exercise of power by Congress; but taking into view the whole opinion of the court and the reasoning by which they have come to that conclusion, I understand them to have decided that inasmuch as a bank is an appropriate means for carrying into effect the enumerated powers of the General Government, therefore the law incorporating it is in accordance with that provision of the Constitution which declares that Congress shall have power "to make all laws which shall be necessary and proper for carrying those powers into execution." Having satisfied themselves that the word "necessary" in the Constitution means "needful," "requisite," "essential," "conductive to," and that "a bank" is a convenient, a useful, and essential instrument in the prosecution of the Government's "fiscal operations," they conclude that to "use one must be within the discretion of Congress" and that "the act to incorporate the Bank of the United States is a law made in pursuance of the Constitution"; "but," say they, "where the law is not prohibited and is really calculated to effect any of the objects intrusted to the Government, to undertake here to inquire into the degree of its necessity would be to pass the line which circumscribes the judicial department and to tread on legislative ground."

The principle here affirmed is that the "degree of its necessity," involving all the details of a banking institution, is a question exclusively for legislative consideration. A bank is constitutional, but it is the province of the Legislature to determine whether this or that particular power, privilege, or exemption is "necessary and proper" to enable the bank to discharge its duties to the Government, and from their decision there is no appeal to the courts of justice. Under the decision of the Supreme Court, therefore, it is the exclusive province of Congress and the President to decide whether the particular features of this act are necessary and proper in order to enable the bank to perform conveniently and efficiently the public duties assigned to it as a fiscal agent, and therefore constitutional, or unnecessary and improper, and therefore unconstitutional.

Without commenting on the general principle affirmed by the Supreme Court, let us examine the details of this act in accordance with the rule of legislative action which they have laid down. It will be found that many of the powers and privileges conferred on it can not be supposed necessary for the purpose for which it is proposed to be created, and are not, therefore, means necessary to attain the end in view, and consequently not justified by the Constitution. . . .

In another point of view this provision is a palpable attempt to amend the Constitution by an act of legislation. The Constitution declares that "the Congress shall have power to exercise exclusive legislation in all cases whatsoever" over the District of Columbia. Its constitutional power, therefore, to establish banks in the District of Columbia and increase their capital at will is unlimited and uncontrollable by any other power than that which gave authority to the Constitution. Yet this act declares that Congress shall not increase the capital of existing banks, nor create other banks with capitals exceeding in the whole $6,000,000. The Constitution declares that Congress shall have power to exercise exclusive legislation over this District "in all cases whatsoever." And this act declares they shall not. Which is the supreme law of the land? This provision can not be "necessary" or "proper" or constitutional unless the absurdity be admitted that whenever it be "necessary and proper" in the opinion of Congress they have a right to barter away one portion of the powers vested in them by the Constitution as a means of executing the rest. . . .

The Government is the only "proper" judge where its agents should reside and keep their offices, because it best knows where their presence will be "necessary." It can not, therefore, be "necessary" or "proper" to authorize the bank to locate branches where it pleases to perform the public service, without consulting the Government, and contrary to its will. The principle laid down by the Supreme Court concedes that Congress can not establish a bank for purposes of private speculation and gain, but only as a means of executing the delegated powers of the General Government. By the same principle a branch bank can not constitutionally be established for other than public purposes. The power which this act gives to establish two branches in any State, without the injunction or request of the Government and for other than public purposes is not "necessary" to the due execution of the powers delegated to Congress. . . .

The principle is conceded that the States can not rightfully tax the operations of the General Government. They can not tax the money of the Government deposited in the State banks, nor the agency of those banks in remitting it; but will any man maintain that their mere selection to perform this public service for the General Government would exempt the State banks and their ordinary business from State taxation? Had the United States, instead of establishing a bank at Philadelphia, employed a private banker to keep and transmit their funds, would it have deprived Pennsylvania of the right to tax his bank and his usual banking operations? It will not be pretended. . . .

It can not be necessary to the character of the bank as a fiscal agent of the Government that its private business should be exempted from that taxation to which all the State banks are liable, nor can I conceive it "proper" that the substantive and most essential powers reserved by the States shall be thus attacked and annihilated as a means of executing the powers delegated to the General Government. It may be safely assumed that none of those sages who had an agency in forming or adopting our Constitution ever imagined that any portion of the taxing power of the States not prohibited to them nor delegated to Congress was to be swept away and annihilated as a means of executing certain powers delegated to Congress.

If our power over means is so absolute that the Supreme Court will not call in question the constitutionality of an act of Congress the subject of which "is not prohibited, and is really calculated to effect any of the objects intrusted to the Government," although, as in the case before me, it takes away powers expressly granted to Congress and rights scrupulously reserved to the States, it becomes us to proceed in our legislation with the utmost caution. Though not directly, our own powers and the rights of the States may be indirectly legislated away in the use of means to execute substantive powers. We may not enact that Congress shall not have the power of exclusive legislation over the District of Columbia, but we may pledge the faith of the United States that as a means of executing other powers it shall not be exercised for twenty years or forever. We may not pass an act prohibiting the States to tax the banking business carried on within their limits, but we may, as a means of executing our powers over other objects, place that business in the hands of our agents and then declare it exempt from State taxation in their hands. Thus may our own powers and the rights of the States, which we can not directly curtail or invade, be frittered away and extinguished in the use of means employed by us to execute other powers. That a bank of the United States, competent to all the duties which may be required by the Government, might be so organized as not to infringe on our own delegated powers or the reserved rights of the States I do not entertain a doubt. Had the Executive been called upon to furnish the project of such an institution, the duty would have been cheerfully performed. In the absence of such a call it was obviously proper that he should confine himself to pointing out those prominent features in the act presented which in his opinion make it incompatible with the Constitution and sound policy. . . .

The bank is professedly established as an agent of the Executive branch of the Government, and its constitutionality is maintained on that ground. Neither upon the propriety of present action nor upon the provisions of this act was the Executive consulted. It has had no opportunity to say that it neither needs nor wants an agent clothed with such powers and favored by such exemptions. There is nothing in its legitimate functions which makes it necessary or proper. Whatever interest or influence, whether public or private, has given birth to this act, it can not be found either in the wishes or necessities of the executive department, by which present action is deemed premature, and the powers conferred upon its agent not only unnecessary, but dangerous to the Government and country.

It is to be regretted that the rich and powerful too often

bend the acts of government to their selfish purposes. Distinctions in society will always exist under every just government. Equality of talents, of education, or of wealth can not be produced by human institutions. In the full enjoyment of the gifts of Heaven and the fruits of superior industry, economy, and virtue, every man is equally entitled to protection by law; but when the laws undertake to add to these natural and just advantages artificial distinctions, to grant titles, gratuities, and exclusive privileges, to make the rich richer and the potent more powerful, the humble members of society—the farmers, mechanics, and laborers—who have neither the time nor the means of securing like favors to themselves, have a right to complain of the injustice of their Government. There are no necessary evils in government. Its evils exist only in its abuses. If it would confine itself to equal protection, and as Heaven does its rains, shower its favors alike on the high and the low, the rich and the poor, it would be an unqualified blessing. In the act before me there seems to be a wide and unnecessary departure from these just principles. . . .

Experience should teach us wisdom. Most of the difficulties our Government now encounters and most of the dangers which impend over our Union have sprung from an abandonment of the legitimate objects of Government by our national legislation, and the adoption of such principles as are embodied in this act. Many of our rich men have not been content with equal protection and equal benefits, but have besought us to make them richer by act of Congress. By attempting to gratify their desires we have in the results of our legislation arrayed section against section, interest against interest, and man against man, in a fearful commotion which threatens to shake the foundations of our Union. It is time to pause in our career to review our principles, and if possible revive that devoted patriotism and spirit of compromise which distinguished the sages of the Revolution and the fathers of our Union. If we can not at once, in justice to interests vested under improvident legislation, make our Government what it ought to be, we can at least take a stand against all new grants of monopolies and exclusive privileges, against any prostitution of our Government to the advancement of the few at the expense of the many, and in favor of compromise and gradual reform in our code of laws and system of political economy.

I have now done my duty to my country. If sustained by my fellow-citizens, I shall be grateful and happy; if not, I shall find in the motives which impel me ample grounds for contentment and peace. . . .

—Andrew Jackson

When asked about the dangers of a presidential veto at the height of the bank battle, Henry Clay sharply replied: "Should Jackson veto it, I shall veto him!"

But he spoke too soon; the president's veto was sustained.

The bitter fight was not yet over, however, for although Old Hickory had won a great victory, the bank retained vast sums of federal funds.

Jackson directed these monies be withdrawn and placed in designated state banks that became widely known as "Jackson's pet banks."

Biddle struck back by tightening the nation's credit, which would lead to great distress in the years ahead.

It was a losing but savage fight.

"The Monster," as Old Hickory labeled it, was finally forced to transform itself into a state bank in Pennsylvania and the Second Bank of the United States and its dictatorial president vanished from the national scene.

Part XIII

Thou great democratic God! Thou who didst pick up Andrew Jackson from the pebbles; who didst hurl him upon a warhorse; who didst thunder him higher than a throne.
                    —Herman Melville in *Moby Dick*

46

Flaming Spirit

THE CLOSING YEARS OF JACKSON'S ADMINISTRATION
would be darkened by the forced removal of the Indians from the southern United States to across the Mississippi River and by the beginning of the long and bloody
Second Seminole War in Florida.

These sad events would leave ugly stains on his own
character and that of the nation he led.

There also would be the growing shadows that foretold
the coming conflict over slavery and the cold financial
winds heralding the Panic of 1837.

But the Great Rebellion would be years away, and the
Panic of 1837 would not burst upon the country until after
Old Hickory had turned the presidency over to his chosen
successor and vice president, Martin Van Buren.

The victor of New Orleans would leave the White House

with a great surge of appreciation and good will from his countrymen.

At the inauguration the tall, straight figure of the sick, silvery haired old man held the attention of the crowds who had come for the installation of President Van Buren.

His friend, Senator Thomas Hart Benton, was led to say, "For once the rising was eclipsed by the setting sun."

Once again back at his beloved Hermitage and Rachel's grave, he resumed the life of the farmer that he always had loved.

The Hermitage was begining to become a national shrine for the common people, who, in spite of the mistakes Jackson had made, instinctively trusted him to the hilt.

It also was a political center for the Democratic Party, which owed its birth and growth to his leadership during the nation's break with its old conservative and aristocratic past.

In spite of his many physical ills: tuberculosis (which had wasted away one lung and damaged the other), headaches, and the dysentery that plagued him still, Old Hickory, with his indomitable will, had time for all his well wishers. He especially had time for the veterans who had served with him in that long in doubt, improbable campaign against the best that mighty England could throw against his polyglot army manning the Mud Ramparts behind the Rodriguez Canal at the Battle of New Orleans.

The end came for the Old General at six o'clock on a peaceful Sunday afternoon as the Tennessee sun lingered on the porticoes of The Hermitage on June 8, 1845.

A day after the burial, Supreme Court Justice John Catron credited Jackson's long career to his magnificent leadership.

The way a thing should be done struck him plainly and he adopted the plan. . . . To the execution he brought a hardy industry, and a sleepless energy, few could equal. . . . But most of all his awful will, stood alone, and was made the will of all he commanded. . . . If he had fallen from the clouds into a city on fire, he woud have been at the head of the extinguishing host in an hour, and would have blown up a palace to stop the fire with as little misgiving as another would have torn down a board shed. In a moment he would have willed it proper—and in ten minutes the thing would have been done. Those who never worked before, who had hardly courage to try, would have rushed to the execution, and applied the match.

"Hence it is," the justice emphasized, "that timid men, and feeble women, have rushed to onslaught when he gave the command—fierce, fearless, and unwavering, for the first time."

Jackson's subsequent incredible career stemmed back to that peacefully quiet noontide of December 23, 1814, when a wild rider dismounted from his lathered horse to rouse the commanding general from his couch of pain in the headquarters of his army in the Rue Royale, New Orleans, with the shocking news that the British Army stood eight miles below the city with no force or obstacle of any kind barring the way to its capture.

A stunned Jackson had sat bolt upright on the edge of his couch asking himself how this could be true.

But it was true enough, confirmed by four of his officers a few moments later.

Listening to their reports with eyes of fire, he wasted no time on useless lamentation, regrets or recriminations.

Rising to his booted feet, his cheeks aflame with the spirit of combat, he smashed his fist down on the plain board table.

"By the Eternal, they shall not sleep on our soil!"

Then in an instant, all cool and calculating, he invited his messengers of doom to share a glass of wine while he sent for his military aides and secretaries.

While awaiting their arrival, he turned to his officers with his decision. "Gentlemen, the British are below. We must fight them tonight."

It was the critical point of the entire campaign.

The surprisers would be surprised. Perhaps they might be destroyed.

The attacker would be counterattacked. Hopefully, the havoc would be immense.

It would be delivered in utter darkness.

It would give Jackson command of the battle.

It also would give him command of the battles that were to follow, leading up to the climax of Pakenham's great assault on the Mud Ramparts Line of January 8, 1815.

England's supreme effort in the war would be thrown back in utter defeat.

Two British generals would meet death upon the field.

Jackson would be the Hero of New Orleans.

Elected seventh president of the United States, he would be immortalized in his credo: "Our Union: It must be preserved!"